The Bishop

Also From Skye Warren

Endgame trilogy
The Pawn
The Knight
The Castle

Masterpiece duet
The King
The Queen

Trust Fund duet
Survival of the Richest
The Evolution of Man

North Security trilogy
Overture
Concerto
Sonata

A Modern Fairy Tale duet
Beauty and the Professor
Falling for the Beast

STANDALONES
Audition
Escort
Anti Hero

For a complete listing of Skye Warren books, visit
www.skyewarren.com/books

The Bishop
A Tanglewood Novella

By Skye Warren

1001 DARK NIGHTS
PRESS

The Bishop
A Tanglewood Novella
By Skye Warren

1001 Dark Nights
Copyright 2020 Skye Warren
ISBN: 978-1-970077-63-6

Foreword: Copyright 2014 M. J. Rose
Published by 1001 Dark Nights Press, an imprint of Evil Eye Concepts, Incorporated

Acknowledgments from the Author

Thank you so much to Liz, Jillian, and M.J. for inviting me to join the 1,001 family of authors. It feels warm and cozy here.

Sign up for the 1001 Dark Nights Newsletter
and be entered to win a Tiffany Key necklace.

There's a contest every month!

Go to www.1001DarkNights.com to subscribe.

**As a bonus, all subscribers can download
FIVE FREE exclusive books!**

One Thousand and One Dark Nights

Once upon a time, in the future…

I was a student fascinated with stories and learning.
I studied philosophy, poetry, history, the occult, and
the art and science of love and magic. I had a vast
library at my father's home and collected thousands
of volumes of fantastic tales.

I learned all about ancient races and bygone
times. About myths and legends and dreams of all
people through the millennium. And the more I read
the stronger my imagination grew until I discovered
that I was able to travel into the stories... to actually
become part of them.

I wish I could say that I listened to my teacher
and respected my gift, as I ought to have. If I had, I
would not be telling you this tale now.
But I was foolhardy and confused, showing off
with bravery.

One afternoon, curious about the myth of the
Arabian Nights, I traveled back to ancient Persia to
see for myself if it was true that every day Shahryar
(Persian: شهريار, "king") married a new virgin, and then
sent yesterday's wife to be beheaded. It was written
and I had read that by the time he met Scheherazade,
the vizier's daughter, he'd killed one thousand
women.

Something went wrong with my efforts. I arrived in the midst of the story and somehow exchanged places with Scheherazade – a phenomena that had never occurred before and that still to this day, I cannot explain.

Now I am trapped in that ancient past. I have taken on Scheherazade's life and the only way I can protect myself and stay alive is to do what she did to protect herself and stay alive.

Every night the King calls for me and listens as I spin tales. And when the evening ends and dawn breaks, I stop at a point that leaves him breathless and yearning for more. And so the King spares my life for one more day, so that he might hear the rest of my dark tale.

As soon as I finish a story... I begin a new one... like the one that you, dear reader, have before you now.

Prologue

Death has a sound. There's a rattle in her breathing that wasn't there this morning. I move the knight over my pawns, which has been my opening move since forever. We can pretend like this is a regular day. Momma studies the board with a look of concentration, even though she makes the same move—her king-side pawn two spaces forward. It's something I can count on, that move, and it doesn't let me down. Her hand trembles as it falls back to the couch.

Death has a smell. There's the cough medicine that's dribbled some on her dress. The deep infection that wheezes out on every breath. We've been living in this world for days, weeks. Years, really. Momma gets sick a few times every winter, but it hit her harder this year. The same thing that made her think slow made her immune system weak.

I move my queen side pawn forward, mostly because I want her to react.

She captures my pawn.

It would almost be enough to convince me everything's normal, if it weren't for Poppa watching us from the kitchen. His eyes are rimmed red. There are a hundred orange bottles spread out across the table. None of the pills and ointments are working. Not anymore.

We move a few pieces, taking up strategic locations across the board. There was a time she could read and write. She knew what every medicine in those bottles does, but I was too young to remember. Mostly I know her this way—quiet and focused and simple. She needs help getting dressed and showering every day. Maybe the other kids in school would think that's weird, but I don't really care. Poppa's out on calls most nights, so who else will do it?

Death has a face, and it's not even my mother's expression of concentration.

It's Poppa, with his shoulders hunched over, his eyes leaking. It looks like failure.

I push my bishop forward, angle him so he's facing her queen. I've never had to go easy on her. She needs help doing the buttons in order, but she never stopped being able to play chess.

As soon as my finger leaves the little knob on the wooden bishop I see my mistake. Her castle's already in the middle of the board. I was so focused on the crack in her defenses that I missed it. I hold my breath, because the boys at school would be watching me. We don't play chess. It's strictly poker with lunch money as the bet while we're on the bus.

Before I can react she's reaching out to move the castle, to knock my bishop out of the way, to move my piece to the side—in that fast, efficient movement of someone ready to make their next move.

"Good one!" The words bubble out of me, and I'm laughing. It's too loud.

Except her hand falls to the side. Her arm isn't trembling anymore. It's limp. The wooden piece rolls out of her hand and softly, softly onto the carpet.

My laugh stops. All of a sudden. Her eyes are closed, as if she's sleeping. "Momma?"

"No, goddamn you. *No.*" Poppa's never really angry, but he looks like a stranger. He lunges across the room and knocks over the chess board. The pieces spill into my lap, and I jump back. He grabs her in a tight hug, and he's making this sound—it's crying. He's crying. Momma's head wobbles on her neck like she's one of those figures you put in a car.

My stomach cramps hard, and I bend over, unable to breathe.

Death has a feeling, and it's cold. Cold enough that I start shivering.

Poppa shakes her, more rough than I've ever seen him. "*You don't get to take her.*"

He's wrong, though. It doesn't matter how much medicine you have or how much you want something. Doesn't matter how much you fight. Death always wins. It took her on a sunny afternoon, as quick and quiet as swiping a piece off the board.

Chapter One

Anders

Chaos. The painting looks like chaos. Is it still called a painting if there are nails sticking out? There's also a button, a burnt match, an old house key. It reminds me of a picture where you're supposed to spy certain items. A puzzle, though it probably means something deeper. The inconstancy of man or some shit. One particular inconstant man comes to stand beside me.

"What's it supposed to mean?" I murmur without looking to the side.

"I don't know and don't care," comes the cavalier response. "It should go for a pretty penny, which is the only thing that makes it interesting."

"Not as pretty as the bishop." Paintings. Jewels. There are even a few genuine Victorian gowns worn by some long-dead wealthy British people. We're standing among millions of dollars—currently in the form of art. After the auction next week that art will be transformed into cash.

Damon Scott gives a quiet laugh. "Not nearly."

"Nice turnout."

Tanglewood high society came out in full force to be seen as a serious contender at the auction benefiting migrant children. Tinkling laughter shimmers in the air. Men and women mingle. It emphasizes how still the two of us stand, how serious.

"Are you sure you want to sell it?" Damon asks, thought the chess piece has already been appraised and announced. It's already pictured in high-gloss photography in the auction program.

"Of course."

The Den is part social club, part underground hub for illicit activity. Countless paintings and priceless sports memorabilia have been sold between these walls. There was even a noteworthy auction involving the virginity of a woman. The bloodied history of this chess piece fits right in.

Damon frowns. "It's a family heirloom. If you need money—"

Christ. Damon Scott is one of the few men I consider a friend. I can't bear the thought of him offering me a loan. Or worse—a gift. I don't need the goddamn money, but it's easier if he thinks I do. "With the old man gone, there's no family left. So there's no reason to keep it."

A whistle. "That's cold, even coming from you."

I have something of a reputation. In an emergency room, being calm and controlled is an asset. In the regular world people look at me like I'm a monster. Well, maybe I am. The old man thought so. He never understood that a blue flame burns the hottest. "Is it wrong to care about the money?"

"Everyone cares about the money, Anders. That's the one human constant. Anyone who says otherwise is either lying or drinking their own goddamn Kool-Aid."

He walks away, leaving me to study the dark swaths alone. Maybe the painting is about money, then. I'd rather be on call tonight, or at least buried in a stack of books, but I have to see this through. All the way to the bitter end.

Family. It's an interesting concept for someone known as the Ice Man through med school. Pops sent me a few hundred bucks every month. We weren't close, but I respected his wishes about the chess piece. The second his heart stopped, the promise was over.

With my hands in the pockets of my slacks, I stroll to the next painting. This one's a mixture of red and pink. It looks like a giant Valentine's card. Made by a three-year-old. Christ.

The next painting catches my eye.

It's simpler, with thick black strokes at the bottom, a grey wash above it, and metallic gold sprinkled in to the top. It reminds me of the city at night, with its beauty and danger. A small signature in the bottom right corner reads N. Lhuirs.

A slender woman studies the same painting. "Do you like it?" she asks, a musical lilt softening the consonants in her words.

"Better than the other ones. Is it supposed to be a city?"

"It's whatever you'd like it to be."

I give her a sideways look, which lets me see her aristocratic profile and snug black dress. I wouldn't be a man if I didn't admire the way it pushes up her tits. I think most of us trapped in tuxedos appreciate the women in slinky dresses more than what's on the walls. "You're one of those."

"One of what?" She sounds amused.

"One of the people who think art means anything. Which really means nothing, doesn't it?"

"Very Orwellian. However, I don't think the viewer can be discounted from the equation. If the artist wanted to keep control over the canvas, he should have kept it in his studio. Once it's on display, it's meant to be seen, meant to be interpreted—even in unexpected ways."

Her voice flows over me like cool water on a burning summer afternoon. I want her to keep talking, even if it's about something as useless as art. "I like things that have clear answers. Mathematical equations. Scientific hypotheses. I like things to make sense."

"What about right and wrong? Do those have clear answers?"

It seems like she's actually interested in what I have to say. As if she's actually been wondering about this. It's a kind of seduction, this challenge. An intellectual lure that I'm swimming toward hard and fast. Flirtation I could have resisted easily. A logical proof is impossible to ignore.

Which means she's dangerous, of course.

"There are moral absolutes," I say. "Don't you think so?"

"Yes," she says, a little sadly. "I think so."

"Do you work for Damon Scott?"

Her eyebrows raise. Dark eyes shine with twinkling lights, as glorious as the gold flecks on the dark painting. "What makes you think that?"

"You know about art."

"Not really. Not about this painting. It suits you, however. There's something very contained about it, as if it holds mysteries that we can only see in shadow." Deep ruby lips make me imagine what we could do in those shadows. My cock hardens. It's a wholly inappropriate reaction to have in a crowded room. And completely out of my control. I've seen countless female bodies in my time as a physician. Some of them have belonged to models and athletes. Some of them have belonged to sorority girls. None of them have scraped my insides, waking up a hunger long asleep.

"If you don't work for the Den, you must be a buyer."

"My bank account couldn't cover even the smallest thing in this auction." She wears a private smile, as if she's thinking of a joke only she knows. "I'm not even sure I can afford a drink."

"And you claim I'm the one holding mysteries."

A soft laugh. Her smile makes my blood warm, makes my heart speed up. I've seen human bodies in every state of health and illness. It's been a long time since one affected me at all. "Perhaps I'm like you, selling something, waiting to see how much it will bring."

Surprise is a pleasant distraction. "How did you know I'm selling something?"

"The chess piece. You're watching it."

"Maybe I want to buy it."

"You haven't spared a single glance at the small piece in the case. Nor have you gone close enough to admire it. Instead you're more interested in the men who circle it like vultures."

Damn. The woman's too perceptive. "Not a buyer. Not a seller. Not working for the auction house. If you won't tell me what you are, at least tell me your name."

"Maybe I'm like the painting—open for interpretation." Voices turn loud behind us, and she turns in surprise, her dark eyes wary. I look back too, in time to hear the proximity alarm go off.

Someone's standing too close to the rectangular display case that holds my chess piece. Everyone backs up, laughing, half-drunk—more than half-drunk, really. Fully drunk. A man trips over himself, hands up, looking both chagrined and proud, as if he's just completed a dare from his friends.

This is what happens when frat boys graduate. They turn into hedge fund managers and financial analysts with more money than sense.

The chess piece sits placidly on its red velvet pillow. It's survived nine hundred years. A handful of clumsy assholes at a preview party aren't going to change that.

I look back to my mystery woman. The place beside the painting is empty.

She's gone.

Chapter Two

Anders

Afternoon heat leans into the curtains. I open my eyes to a blank white ceiling. I turn my face toward a blank white room. It's a spare existence, but it suits me. I don't need luxury. I don't want it. A vibration of my phone. That must be what woke me.

Breech, it says, with an address.

A quick shower that also serves as an antiseptic. I cleaned up after tending the gunshot victim last night, but it doesn't hurt to be careful. I don't look forward to attending births. The stakes of failure are too high. Modern medicine hasn't eliminated the risk to mothers or infants. In fact, some of the interventions actually increase the risk. That's exactly the kind of fucked-up progress I've learned to expect from the world. And proof that even science doesn't always make sense.

The Den is a private club in one of the worst parts of town. That's why it's the perfect place for me to rent a room. It takes only a few minutes to arrive at the house in question. People line the foyer and fill the living room. Wide eyes watch me with hope and suspicion. They trust their midwife, not me, but Rosa knows to contact me for something as serious as breech.

I find her upstairs in a small room, the damp of sweat heavy in the air. The young mother pants in the bed, her eyes glazed with pain or delirium, her belly swollen.

Rose gestures to a basin of hot water, where I wash my hands again. "They called me this morning," she says. "I was with another child. This is the first time I've seen her."

Hell. The chances of maternal death shoot through the roof when there's no prenatal care. A growling sound escapes me. "She needs to be in a hospital."

"You know why she can't," Rosa snaps.

That's my agreement with her. I'm not supposed to mention the hospital, even if it's best for the patients. Even if they die in my care. If I force the issue once, she'll never call me again. Which means more people could die. It's a hell of a catch 22.

What about right and wrong? Do those have clear answers?

No, they don't.

This woman can't go to the hospital because the immigration officials would take her into custody. They would make her give birth handcuffed to a goddamn hospital bed. They'd take the baby away from her, and she might never see him again. It's not a choice; it's a matter of life or death.

I kneel by her side, because it's the least I can do before I shove my hand into her vagina. "I'm Dr. Anders Sorenson. I'm going to check on the baby, okay?"

She doesn't answer. I'm not sure she's aware of anything except the inner turmoil of her body. I move between her legs and perform an examination. "Where's the father?" I mutter to Rosa, thinking of those solemn faces below.

"With the other children. This isn't her first time."

Because she might get taken into custody. If it comes to that, they want the father to stay with the other children. It's a sad fucking day when families have to separate to stay together.

I pull my hand out. "He's coming out."

"She asked to keep the baby alive," Rosa whispers. "No matter what."

They always ask to keep the baby alive. Williams was wrong. Money isn't the one human constant. It's this. The love of a mother for her child. Sacrifice. That's what I can count on. That's what makes sense.

I glance at my phone, which sits face up on a side table in the cramped room. Delivering a breech baby is more art than science. The skill isn't passed on these days, but it used to be the only choice. We'll pretend it's the Roaring '20s. "He's coming out. In the next five hours.

If not, then I'm driving her to the hospital myself."

It doesn't take five hours. It takes six.

Another three hours to deliver the placenta and stitch up the mother while Rosa makes sure the baby latches. The father and children arrive to the small apartment as I'm leaving, covered in blood and amniotic fluid that only a shower in boiling water will fix. I pick up my phone on the way down the stairs, glancing at the screen. Twenty-six messages. Twelve voicemails.

I press *play* on the first one. "The chess piece. It's gone."

Chapter Three

Anders

Slanting rays of yellow light blind me. My pulse beats hard and fast. Heavy doors creak as I pull them open. The Den looks empty. Then my eyes adjust. There are people lined up in the shadows.

Damon stands in front of them like a general examining his army. And finding them lacking. He greets me with a hard handshake. "Everyone who worked last night. The caterers, the cleaners. Even the poor bastard who had to fix the toilet after enough of the women taking cocaine took a shit."

Modern day servants. They remind me of the people lining the living room in the house, wary and watchful. Those people feared me because I'm an outsider, because one call to the authorities could tear apart their lives. These people fear me because they know me. At least, they know my reputation. I wouldn't put it past Damon to use it to his advantage, to threaten that I'd kill them if they had anything to do with the theft. It wouldn't necessarily be a lie.

The pillar stands where it should. The red velvet pillow remains inside. The glass case covers it neatly. Except there's no carved chess piece inside. There's no redemption for my family inside. My chest constricts, until it's hard to breathe. In public, no less. I cross my arms over my chest as if to contain the panic. It doesn't help. "Walk me through it."

"The chess piece was there when the cleaning crew left last night. We can see it on the video. The lights turn off, everything's dark. In the morning it's gone."

"What else?"

"Was taken? Nothing."

Rage rises in my chest, but I force it down. "There are countless works of art. Antique coins. Jewels. You're telling me they're all accounted for."

"Every piece."

"How did this happen?"

"The security system wasn't compromised."

"It hasn't been compromised? This is the definition of compromised."

"I mean it didn't alarm. Our cameras didn't catch anything. My men at the exits and on the roof across the street didn't see a damn thing. He's like a ghost, whoever this was." Damon runs a hand over his face. "I'm not making excuses. Of course I'm responsible."

I press my lips into a firm line. It's the kind of honor you wouldn't expect from anyone else in the criminal underworld. It's standard operating procedure for Damon Scott. He'll probably pay me the full million dollar valuation for the chess piece out of his own pocket. That doesn't solve my problem. This was never about the money. "Don't worry about it."

"Believe me. I'm fucking worried about it." He glances toward the back office where his wife Penny usually spends her days bent over a notebook full of numbers and mathematical symbols. He has more than enough money to throw an auction. For him she's more valuable than his whole empire.

"I'm glad you're okay." Because if she'd gotten hurt during a break-in, a break-in for *my* chess piece, for my revenge mission, the guilt would have been unbearable. It would have been something no amount of free baby deliveries would have made up for.

"We'll find the bishop. That's a goddam promise." He nods toward the row of soldiers. "In the meantime I kept them here so you could question them yourself."

It's worth trying, because this burglary was clearly not about money. They could have taken art or coins or jewels for that. There are very few people in the world who would be interested in this piece. Any of them with the resources to stage a successful burglary could afford to bid in the auction.

Who wants the piece but needs privacy more? Exactly the person I'm seeking.

If I don't follow the trail I might lose them forever.

A row of men and women, each of them looking nervous, each of them with their own weak points. I could question them for hours. Learn their darkest secrets. Would it bring me closer to the chess piece? I'm less interested in who's lined up; instead I want to know about the woman who's missing.

How to describe her? *Like the city at night. Beauty and danger.*

Beautiful. "There was a woman," I say. "Five four. Slender. Dark hair and brown eyes. Wearing a black dress with lace and long sleeves. I want a name and an address."

* * * *

Penny

Damon walks into the room, bringing with him the thundercloud he's had since he was informed the chess piece disappeared. There are notes from a professor of mathematics waiting for my response, but I set them aside in a stack for later, where my cat quickly finds her next napping place. Damon has torn apart every man and woman running security, every bartender, servant. Even the woman who bakes the bourbon croissants at the bakery down the street got the third degree. That was before he even called Anders. I know Damon wanted to find the piece before it came to that.

He flings himself onto the leather armchair by the fire. I approach him from behind, rubbing his shoulders. There are too many knots for my fingers to make much progress.

"Must be hard," I say softly.

"What?" He's irritable, my man who always has a blithe remark.

"Not being perfect."

His shoulders turn to stone for a brief, tense moment. Then he crosses one leg over the other, feigning nonchalance. "I want the Den to be safe. That's a reasonable expectation."

I circle the armchair and place my knee on the cushion between his legs. "The world isn't safe, Damon. At the end of the day, no one was hurt. Only one thing was taken. Things can be replaced."

"It's 900 years old. Not exactly found at Walmart."

I press a kiss to the corner of his mouth. He's already noticing my breasts rubbing against him. He may be grumpy and upset—and because I know him, I can tell, *afraid*—but he's still a man. "It's bad," I agree, "especially if Anders needs the money. I assume you offered to replace it."

"He told me no, which is just bullshit. It's my responsibility."

"Then again, I'm not sure he does need the money."

"Why else would he sell it?"

I rest back on his lap, laughing a little. "The one human constant? I'm not sure it's money. What about family? What about redemption? What about revenge?"

His eyebrows knit. "Revenge? You mean his mother?"

My smile slips. Martha Sorenson was basically a legend in the west side of Tanglewood. She came from one of the wealthy families. Got a medical degree, but instead of marrying a surgeon and settling down to raise babies, she went to work for the poor of the city. Her family disowned her, but that didn't stop her. "Where else do you think they'd get a priceless antique like that? It's not likely Mr. Sorenson picked it up on one of his night calls."

Martha Sorenson was attacked on one of her nightly calls to help someone. She was raped, beaten, and left for dead. Only, she didn't die. Her husband found her and nursed her back to health, but she was never the same. She could never practice medicine again—or even read or write.

"So it came to him through his mother's side. How does putting it for sale help get revenge?"

"Presumably he has a reason to believe the person who hurt her wants that piece. I don't know the answer, but I don't think he needs cash. I don't think he wants it, either. He lives like a monk. What would he spend it on? A new car? No."

"Maybe a hit man. For this revenge he wants so badly."

I drop my forehead to his, as if I can fuse into him, protect him from everything bad that might ever happen. The Sorensons are the terrifying possible ending to every love story. Mr. Sorenson continued to care for the poor after his wife's attack, after her eventual death, but he never smiled again.

"Would you?" I ask softly. "Hire someone? Or would you do it yourself?"

Large hands tighten on my hips, holding me flush against his, hard enough that his erection feels like iron at my core. I know that what will come next is an affirmation of life in the most carnal way. His eyes study mine, sorrowful for even the possibility. "I would destroy the whole world."

Chapter Four

Anders

The underside of a moss-damp rock. The insides of a rotten stump. The Rose and Crown Motel attracts those who slink away from the light. It breeds violence and decay. The idea of the mystery woman here makes me uneasy. Men will assume the worst about her. They'll think she's for sale. They may not even ask how much before taking what they want.

Of course, she might be a prostitute.

She also might be the thief who stole my chess piece.

A series of inquiries through the fabric of criminals and lowlifes in Tanglewood led me to this motel. That's a generous word, motel. It implies there would be a place to rent rooms, for one thing. Instead there's a phone number written in black marker across a dark window. A pair of cats yowls their battle cries from somewhere close. A woman in fishnet leans against the broken brick. She smiles at me, revealing black spaces where teeth should be. "Do you good for twenty?" she says, her voice slurring. I really shouldn't, but my mind can't help but diagnose her ailments. A disturbing number are visible. I can guess the rest. I pull a hundred dollar bill from my wallet and hold it out.

Her fingers tremble as she reaches for it. I don't let go.

"A woman. Dark hair. Lush body. A voice that sounds like music."

She licks her cracked lips. "You aren't gonna hurt her?"

For years I've lived by that edict—do no harm. It came to me as easy as breathing. There's only one thing that could make me break the rule. "Not if she gives me back what's mine."

A brief pause. "Room forty-nine."

I step over sleeping bodies and around used needles in the breezeway. Murky water ripples gently in an ancient rectangular pool, hiding trash and vegetation and possibly more than one dead body. A palm tree looks disturbingly cheerful in the silhouette of the sky. It took me twenty-four hours, almost a lifetime when it comes to a theft involving a million dollars.

The sensation inside me is almost… hope. That she would be long gone. I don't want to hurt her. *Do no harm.* As easy as breathing, unless you made a promise on your father's deathbed.

I sense the difference before I turn the corner. A disturbance. Danger.

The door to room forty-nine stands open an inch.

No one would leave their door open here. No one would leave their door unlocked in the entire west side of Tanglewood. This isn't the goddamn Little House on the Prairie.

No one would leave a million-dollar chess piece unguarded.

I don't carry a gun. It's a matter of principle. What you carry, you might use. When you use a gun, no matter how good your aim, people tend to die. Which means I'm walking in unprotected. Not harming people increases my own likelihood of dying. Such is the way of the animal kingdom.

A bed in disarray. White sheets. A bedspread with faded pink roses half on the floor. Cigarette burns on worn carpet. That's what I can see in the sliver through the doorway. I push it open another two inches. Someone searched this place. The table leans on its side. A thin cushion has been cut through, spilling yellow foam. Clothes lie scattered around a duffel bag, as if there was a small explosion.

I step into the room with caution. Silence. Stillness. I'm alone here.

Or the person in the room with me is dead. Both sensations feel about the same. More things torn apart, flipped over. I reach the bathroom. Feminine lotions and makeup criss-cross the counter. No dead bodies. Relief flickers inside me. I've learned to stay detached. That mother from before. The baby. They die often enough that I can't get attached. But if I'd found the woman, the body full of vibrancy dead in this motel room, it would have hurt. Even knowing she's probably a criminal, and most likely working with the men who killed my parents, doesn't mute the strange warmth I have for her.

A sound, like a kitten. No breathing. Not even my heart can beat in the second I listen for intruders. Have they come back to search more? Then I hear it, the haggard breathing of a human fighting to live. I've heard the sound enough to recognize it. I turn the corner, my senses on alert to danger, but there's only one body in the alley.

I bend and check her pulse. Thready.

"Can you hear me? Wake up, sweetheart."

There's muck on her from the slick gravel. It's muddied her hair, her face. I brush some of it away to reveal small cuts from where the pebbles grated her skin. There's an ugly bruise on her cheekbone. Somewhere lower there's blood. I'm not sure whether it's some doctor's instinct that tells me that or the metallic scent of blood. It's coming from a deep gash above her left clavicle. I tear off my T-shirt and press it against the wound.

She moans in protest.

"I know. It's going to hurt." A brief patdown reveals no broken bones, though the pain can almost be worse this way than a clean cut. "Wake up for me."

Her eyelids flutter. And then her breath stops.

For one terrible moment the alleyway's in complete silence.

I shake her—too rough. "No, goddamn you. *No.*"

The body wants to avoid pain. It'll do anything, sometimes—even drift away slowly. Even die. I'm not going to let that happen. I refuse to let that happen.

You don't get to take her.

Chapter Five

Natalie

The pain is far away.

It bursts through my awareness like flickering firelight—sparks that fade into the night. I don't want to get closer. It will burn me if I do. It's safer in the shadows of my consciousness, where I don't have to think about what happened or wonder where I am now.

A flare of color in the burn, enough to make me gasp.

Something's dragging me out of the dark.

Something's tearing my arm out of its socket.

Someone's squeezing my ribs until it feels like they'll crack.

A moan cuts through the heavy black. It raises the hair on my arms. It sends a chill down my spine. Suffering. Grief. An animal that should be put out of its misery. *Wake up now*, says the darkness. I don't know how it can speak, this faceless void. Is it death?

You have to drink something. If I don't get liquids into you soon I'll have to take you to a hospital, and somehow I think you'd like that even less than I would.

Darkness sounds like… a man.

Something cool touches my lips. My head is tipped back. Liquid slides across my tongue. My throat swallows without my permission. Dew in the early morning. Warm rain in the spring. It breathes life into me, despite my fervent wish for oblivion. The water wakes up every throbbing, broken part of my body. It seizes every muscle. My stomach.

My throat. The last drop makes me choke.

"Easy." Strong hands help me turn to the side. I cough against a pillow, every spasm wrenching something open in my chest. "Breathe. In and out. There you go. Keep breathing."

When I was lying in that alleyway I decided I'd had enough of breathing, enough of living. Part of me resents this man for taking that choice away. It's impossible to take stock of my injuries. Every inhale brings a new hurt. Every exhale makes me dizzy with exhaustion.

The darkness wraps its tentacles around me. It drags me down.

* * * *

The first thing in my head isn't a thought—it's pounding.

The rhythmic beat of a hymn. My mother singing Hosanna. She doesn't like to go every week. Mostly she goes for appearances, but she does love the music. Every week we'd flip open the hymnal to see what we'd be singing.

Louder and louder and louder. It's no longer a sound; it's a thumping in my veins. It's slamming through my body on every quarter beat, heavy notes echoing in my joints.

I'm alive. The awareness comes only a split second before I remember the fear—the certainty that I would die in that alleyway. Stinking. Dark. Alone. I must not have been entirely alone. Even muted with agony I know I'm no longer on pavement. A twitch of my pinky finger. It's all I can venture. I'm rewarded with an ache that resounds through my arm, my shoulder, my entire body. My sensory awareness catches up. The sheets are cool to the touch. Soft. Softer than my motel bed? Yes. Which means I'm not safe. Does he have me? Panic shoots up my spine, followed by searing pain. I have to get away from here. I have to—

"Hey. Take it easy. You aren't going anywhere."

The words could be a threat. Of course they are. The whole world is a threat. I'm trapped in my own bruised body. I can't even open my eyes. They're glued together. I force them apart. A low moan fills my ears, and in a moment of horror, I realize it's coming from me.

"You're determined to pull those stitches, aren't you?"

It's not *him*, but that doesn't mean he's trustworthy. The world is full of men determined to take advantage of a situation. As soon as one falls away, another takes his place. My mother didn't believe in God. She believed in scarred wooden pews and colorful stained glass, because they were things you could touch. She believed in the peace you could find in a fleeting song.

No one could take that away. *Hosanna in the highest…*

"Easy." The voice is closer now, more rumbly. "Easy now. You're a mess of bruises right now. By rights you should be in a hospital hooked up to a nice comfortable morphine drip. Instead you're stuck with me. Don't make it worse for yourself."

It's not his words that force me to stop. It's the blinding pain. It steals the air in the room. It makes everything feel dark and murky, as if I'm about to pass out.

"There you go. In and out. Breathe in and out."

Simple instructions. My mind follows them without thinking. It occurs to me that this could be intentional—to make me dependent on him, to coax me into following directions. Start with small things like breathing. Once I'm in deep enough he can make me do anything, right? Like steal a chess piece. Except I already did that. My stomach clenches. "Where—" I force the words through painful, cracked lips. "Where am I?"

"Somewhere a lot cleaner than that alley. Smells better, too."

The memory comes back to me in a rush of blurry fear—the slick gravel beneath my feet, the sound of heavy breathing behind me. The heavy slam of a large body into mine. I didn't smell anything except the sharp metal tang of blood. "Need to go."

"I don't think you'll be going anywhere. Unless you want an ambulance."

"No." Fear spikes in my stomach. "Please."

"You got something against doctors?"

He'll be looking for me in a hospital. The one who holds my fate in his hands.

Meanwhile this man watches me with eyes an unearthly blue. There's a day's growth on his square jaw. Pale blond hair. He looks like some kind of Nordic god, passing judgment. I don't think I fare well in his scale. Maybe I should call an ambulance.

I might not be safer here at all.

My jaw clenches as a fresh wave of pain overcomes me. "Don't need one."

The Nordic god walks to a side table laden with bottles. He fills a syringe with something clear and ominous. "I think you need one, but you're in luck. Because of all the people who could have found you in that alleyway, it was me."

"I'm fine."

That earns me a quirk of his lips. "You nearly died. Still might."

Still might, if I don't get that chess piece back. "Really. I feel better."

"This is heading straight toward a Monty Python sketch."

Throbbing grows second by second. The pain is almost unbearable. I'm ready to beg for whatever's in that syringe, even though it could be anything. It could be poison. Part of me wants that, too. The sweet relief of being done with it. "I don't trust you."

Then he's leaning over me, that arctic blue gaze only inches away. "I don't trust you either. Now that we have that out of the way, perhaps you can tell me your name."

My eyes narrow. "You first."

"Anders Sorenson. I thought you'd know that. I'm the man you stole from."

That's the only warning I get before a sharp pain stabs my arm. I glance down to see him ease the syringe into place. He holds me steady with his other hand while he presses the liquid into my body. It feels ice cold, the same as his eyes. He makes a sound, one that doesn't have a name. Almost like *tch* sound, and it makes me feel better than any fake assurances could have. It's the sound of someone with empathy, isn't it? I search the hard planes of his face for some proof of that. He's focused as he pulls the needle away and replaces it with a bandage.

He knows I stole the chess piece. Then what will he do to me? And more importantly, why would he give me medicine to ease my suffering if he knows what I've done?

"What's your name?" he says, his gaze intent.

My lips press together. Stubborn, my mother would say. Tears prick my eyes.

"Don't you dare cry. No, goddamn you."

Then again, maybe it's designed to make my pain worse, not better. Maybe it's an instrument of torture, along with the other bottles and needles on the dresser. Except I can already feel the relief as it whips through my veins. I already feel the milky comfort envelop me.

Sleep tugs at my consciousness, making him appear softer than he is.

"What will you do to me?" The question comes out slurred.

"I'm going to get answers," he says, sounding far away. I wonder how I ever thought he might have empathy. His voice is completely devoid of feeling. "You're going to tell me where the chess piece is. You're going to tell me who you're working with. We're going to know each other very well by the end, but for now let's start with one thing: what's your name?"

"Natalie," I whisper, because there's no resistance where I'm floating now. There's no friction. Only a painless expanse that never has to end.

A brush of warmth on my forehead. *A kiss.* "Goodnight, Natalie."

Chapter Six

Natalie

Quiet. That's the first thing I notice. Not the heavy beat of pain. There are still aches and bruises. Something particularly dark in my side, but I can breathe without crying.

Golden light stretches across the ceiling. It's late in the day, but I know without asking that more than a few hours have passed. The memories are disjointed, the pale blue eyes watching me, the shots and the sweet relief. It must have been days since the attack at my motel. It feels like an eternity.

I manage to lift my head to see the rest of the room—it's spacious, larger than I realized in my haze of pain. Aside from the ocean-sized bed I'm in, there's are nightstands and a dresser and armchairs tucked around a fireplace.

A man sleeps in one of the armchairs, his head leaned back against the wing, lips parted. Even from this far away I can see the dark circles under his eyes. I can see the heavy growth of blond scruff on his jaw. He wears a dress shirt and black slacks, both of them rumpled but still somehow formal, especially in contrast to his bare feet on the carpet.

Without the pain or the medicine clouding my mind, I understand more clearly how I came to be here. This is the man at the Den, the man who owned the chess piece. Like he said, this is the man I stole from. And he brought me here to get it back.

I understand more clearly how much danger I'm in.

The door is only a few feet away. Is it locked? That's assuming I can get out of bed without falling on my ass. Even with the pain lessened that's still not a sure bet.

"I wouldn't recommend that." His voice sounds sleep-thickened and rough.

My gaze snaps back to meet his pale blue one. "Why not?"

"A few reasons. Starting with the fact that you'd collapse in less than eight hours without medical care. And ending with the fact that you're naked under that blanket."

A hitch in my breath. Carefully I move my hand enough to confirm what he's saying—there's only warm skin. "You got me naked? When I was asleep? And injured? That's—that's—"

"You're welcome. Unless you would have preferred to sleep in sewage for four days."

Four? My God. I struggle to control my expression, but holy shit. Four days. That chess piece could be halfway to Antarctica by now. I lift the blanket with a still shaky hand, cringing at the shadows of my breasts. He saw this. "Wasn't there someone else who could have... A woman?"

"The hospital would have female nurses, but you said not to take you there." He leans forward and puts his elbows on his knees. Even tired and surely sore, he looks competent. That's terrifying in someone who's my enemy. "Let's get one thing straight. My priority was keeping you alive. My next objective is to find the chess piece. Your naked body was nothing but a means to an end."

He's lying. The thought drifts across my consciousness, curious because it doesn't bother me as much as it should. I'm lying naked in a bed with a man in the room, but it has nothing to do with sex. Except that he thought about it—while washing me, while tending my wounds. There's an allure in having someone take care of me, even someone who hates me. I've been alone for so long.

His blue eyes study my shape beneath the blanket, and I flush with warmth. Embarrassment? Yes. Maybe even some indignation. There's something else...

A hint of attraction that has no place in my life. No place in this room.

"Would it be so bad?" I ask, because everything is a weapon when you're backed into a corner. I've never used sexuality before, but it was only a matter of time. "To notice me as a woman? To desire me as a woman? I find you handsome, too, you know."

His eyes turn sharp as glass. "You want to have sex with me in exchange for that chess piece? That's quite an expensive fuck. Not sure I noticed a gold-plated pussy when I helped you piss."

My cheeks burn. "That's crude."

"Not that I think we'd get that far. I think if I took you up on your offer, you'd pass out within ten minutes. If I wanted an unconscious woman, I'd already have had you."

"Or maybe I'd disarm you instead. I might be out the door in ten minutes."

He glances at the door, looking unconcerned. "I really don't recommend that. There's another man downstairs, and he doesn't have any particular reason to keep you alive."

Of course he isn't alone. Even only seeing the room, the crown molding and the plush carpeting, the ornate wood hearth—everything speaks to money. And money means space. Even if I could get out of the room I'd probably get lost in the maze of the mansion.

He crosses the room to the dresser, preparing another syringe.

"No," I say.

That earns me a derisive glance. "I can see you're hurting."

There's a low throb from pretty much every muscle in my body. A few spikes of pain in my side and my head. It's nothing I can't live with. Nothing I haven't lived with before. "No medicine."

A sigh. "You don't need to put on a brave face."

"I'm not being brave. I'm being practical. If you're going to hurt me I'd rather be fully conscious."

"If I were going to hurt you, I wouldn't bother dulling the effects with medicine."

"I know what you're doing."

He looks amused now. "Do you?"

"You're building up the anticipation. Making me better so that it hits me even harder when you try to tear me down again. It's a mindfuck, a trick, a *performance,* and I'm not falling for it."

He comes to sit on the edge of the bed. The depression he makes causes me to roll toward him before I catch myself. I'm acutely aware that there's only a thin blanket shielding my body from him. Blue eyes flick down to my breasts, to the soft points of my nipples through the fabric, before he meets my gaze. In his eyes I see the promise of what we could have been—if I weren't a few minutes from passing out. If he weren't holding me captive until I give back a chess piece.

The back of his hand strokes my arm. Only a few centimeters apart. A few strands of wool. I can feel the warmth of him. "A performance. Like when I met you in the Den."

My throat tightens. I was already his enemy then, but he didn't know it yet. *Is it supposed to be a city? It's whatever you'd like it to be.* "You saw what you wanted to see."

His sleeves are rolled up, revealing strong forearms with a pale sprinkling of hair. His hands are strong and scarred. Dangerous hands. I've learned to be afraid of men with strength, but it's disconcerting to realize he uses those hands to heal people. "Right. Because you're one of those."

"Yes," I say, letting my frustration bleed through. "One of those people who think art means anything. It can mean expression. It can mean salvation. Right now it means I'm trapped in this bed."

"I like things that have clear answers," he says, repeating his words from that night. "Mathematical equations. Scientific hypotheses. I like things to make sense. In this case, it's only a few words that solve the problem. A location, for starters. Where's the chess piece now?"

I glare at him, pressing my lips together. Part of me knows it's futile to resist. He knows I'm guilty. Except I can't give him what he wants. Having the conversation won't change that.

"How about a name? Who are you working with?"

"I have nothing to tell you."

He lifts his hand to toy with my hair, the dark lock a sharp contrast to his pale, strong fingers. "Black and gold," he murmurs. "Like the city at night. Beauty and danger."

A shiver runs down my spine. It turns into a throb, a heavy beat that grows louder with every second. He wasn't entirely wrong about the sex. I would have passed out within minutes. I'm doing it now. My lids are lowering, even when I'm struggling to stay awake.

A small smile. "Sleep, Natalie. We'll talk later."

No, we won't talk. I have nothing to say to you. Help me, help me. I'm in so deep that I don't know how to get out. No sound escapes my lips. My eyes shutter closed, and he's far away again.

Chapter Seven

Anders

Black hair. Golden skin. I'm downstairs, but I can't escape the haunted look in her dark eyes. God, someone really fucked this woman up. Not only the obvious ways—the contusions and cuts on her body, the bruised ribs. It makes me wonder if they hurt her sexually, too. I didn't see any swelling or redness when I washed her, but that doesn't mean shit.

Would it be so bad? To notice me as a woman? To desire me as a woman? There are a thousand ways men have learned to hurt women, some that don't leave a mark. Like the way she offered to let me fuck her in exchange for letting her go. The horrible part is that I wanted to say yes.

I find you handsome, too, you know.

Christ.

"She still alive?" The question comes from the man already sitting in the library. He stands when I enter and heads to the bar, where he pours us both two fingers of scotch. It probably costs ten thousand dollars a bottle. It's expensive, like the house itself, which he also owns.

I accept the cut-crystal glass with a nod of thanks. "Yes."

He sits in an armchair, inviting me to join him. "Because I'd have a hell of a time explaining that to Avery. She's already distressed, and I don't like her upset in her condition."

"There's nothing to worry about."

"We aren't precisely in the habit of keeping young women in captivity."

I raise my eyebrow at that, so he knows I haven't forgotten how he got together with Avery. He was the winning bid at an auction for her virginity. She wasn't kept here against her will, precisely, but she didn't come for fun either. Circumstances and desperation drove her into his arms, which is the same reason the woman is in the bedroom above me right now.

"She's not being held captive," I say, which is a lie. I wouldn't let her leave, even if she were able. Which she's not. It's captive in every goddamn sense of the word, and Gabriel knows it.

He tips his glass toward me. "Of course, I owe you a few favors."

"Of course." That's an understatement. He owes me his life several times over. People avoid the hospital when the authorities are more dangerous than even a deadly injury. That's true for people dealing with corrupt cops or overzealous ICE agents. Or for people dealing with completely legitimate law enforcement, but who sometimes deal under the table—such as Gabriel Miller.

Gabriel Miller and Damon Scott are the closest things I have to friends. I keep a room in the top floor of the Den as my permanent residence, but I'll disappear for days, weeks, months at a time without telling them. The only reason our friendship works is that they don't give me shit about it. I thought about bringing Natalie to the Den, but whoever she's working with would predict that. They've proven they were able to break the security once already. Even with Damon going apeshit to correct that, I couldn't trust Natalie's safety there.

"There's a limit," he says, studying the glass. "I won't have Avery upset over this. I won't risk her health or the baby because you're on a revenge mission."

I don't show my surprise, but he'll feel it anyway. That's the thing about knowing someone a long time. There's less hiding. "Damon thought I needed money. He almost offered me a loan."

A smirk. "Don't ever take a loan from that bastard. The terms will kill you."

"It was never about the fucking money."

"I think I'd know a man bent on revenge when I saw him. I used to be one. Here's a little advice from someone who's been down that road—there's no changing the past. There's only now and how much you fuck up trying to do the impossible."

If I were a man prone to showing emotion, I'd probably frown or growl or do whatever the alpha men usually do when they're pissed off. Instead I just stare. "That so?"

"Fine, you don't want advice. Of course you don't. They say no man is an island, but you're a goddamn glacier. When are you going to admit you need someone?"

"I need you to stop talking about this."

He studies me over the rim of his glass. "Three days."

I throw back the whiskey. It goes down smooth. Three days to get the information from the woman sleeping above me. Three days not to fuck her beautiful body in that bed.

Three days to avenge my family once and for all.

* * * *

A shower and a cup of coffee do little to revive me, but I don't have time to waste. I'm back in the room when she stirs in bed, turning her head side to side, a notch of pain in between her eyes. I regret letting her talk me out of the Vicodin. Years of practice have left me somewhat inured to people in pain. Callous? Yes. I don't have the ability to feel sad about every patient who's suffering. All I can do is the scientific, logical steps to ease them. Something about her cuts through the heavy canvas, reaching a part of me that can still feel sympathy, a part I didn't know existed anymore.

I sit down beside her, trying to ignore the way her hair spreads across the pillow. It's the same way she would look if her body were under mine, spread open, taking me again and again. I'm sick for wanting her even when she's clearly hurting—but then I've been sick for a long time. Unlike my patients, mine is the kind of sick that scientific, logical steps can do nothing to cure. It goes soul deep.

A low moan that makes the hair on my arms rise.

I shouldn't touch her, not without a clear medical reason. I know that, but somehow I'm running my palm over her forehead, trying to soothe her, even though nothing about me should calm her. She moves restlessly beneath the blanket, her eyelids fluttering.

"Shhh," I say, my throat tight with emotion I shouldn't have. "You're safe."

That's a lie. She's not safe in this room. She's not safe from me.

Maybe she knows, because she doesn't settle. Instead her eyes press together hard. Her head thrashes on the pillow. Her legs move beneath the covers, and I tense, knowing she might pull those stitches in her arm right out. There are plenty of bruises from the beating, some cuts that I sterilized and glued shut. Only one cut needed stitches. A line three inches across her clavicle. The scar will be thin and small and hideable under clothes—but it will always be there, a testament to that night. A testament to her involvement with dangerous men. I think a man who'd hit a woman should be shot. Regardless, I can't claim any moral high ground. Not as long as I keep her in this room.

She moves more, with urgency, with agitation. A nightmare? Physical pain from not having an injection? Either way, I can't watch her suffer. I gently shake her awake, careful not to touch any of her bruises.

Her lashes lift. Her gaze is still unfocused. She's half in the dream world, and it's not a pretty dream. There is conflict and fear in those dark depths. Demons, too.

Slowly she comes awake. "Anders."

"So you do know my name." It's a start. Proof that she knew who I was all along, even back at the Den. I didn't doubt that, but maybe now we can move forward. My information wasn't in the auction program. The seller was listed as anonymous.

She closes her eyes on a sigh. "I was supposed to get close to you. Seduce you. If I got you to trust me, I could get the chess piece. Then suddenly you were selling it, and I had to move fast. I figured it would be better that way—better if you knew me."

Every cell in my body rebels at the idea of not knowing her. Even finding her this way, as a thief, as a traitor, as the woman working with my enemies, I'm still glad it happened. Strange but true. "Where is the chess piece now?"

She shakes her head, a gesture of helplessness more than refusal.

I should push her harder. She's already opened up to me. I know more than I did before. She's admitting planning and complicity. She's admitting she stole it; this is when I should press my advantage. Once I know where the chess piece is, I won't need to keep her locked up anymore.

Well, that's the problem, isn't it? I tell myself silently, my internal voice mocking. Once I know where the chess piece is, I won't have an excuse to keep her with me. I've never cared much for money. It's easy not to care when you have more than you need. I've never cared about cars or big houses. I've never been greedy before. The sensation is foreign and real. I'm greedy for more of her secrets, ones that don't even have to do with me or the chess set or the bastards she's helping.

The bed might as well be as big an ocean—that's how small she looks. That's how adrift. Her eyes reflect defeat as she watches me, probably waiting for me to pounce. I should lean over her, intimidate her with my size, maybe threaten her to speed things along. It wouldn't have to be overt. This woman understands nuance. I could know what I need to in a matter of minutes.

Instead I turn away from her. I stride into the bathroom, with its faux-antique copper handle and shiny white marble. The faucet pours water into the gleaming tub. I stare at the swirl of steaming water. What the hell am I doing? I barely know this woman. It doesn't make any sense to throw away plans decades old for a nice fuck. There's no chance of anything more than that, not with a woman I already know is a thief.

Chapter Eight

Natalie

I have no reason to trust this man.

I also have no choice but to trust him. I rely on him for everything at this moment—for food and shelter. For security. The low throb in my body is a constant, steady reminder that I need his help. I expected him to push his advantage. He could have made me betray everything. He still might, but apparently that's not on the agenda right now.

He comes back into the bedroom, his sleeves rolled up, his hands glistening from the water I hear rushing in the next room. His expression has morphed into one of severe professionalism. His eyes look cold enough to make me shiver. "Bath time."

My heart thuds against my ribs. "Excuse me?"

"I used a washcloth when you got here, but you were too out of it to hold your head up in a tub. Now that you're conscious and not high, there's no better time."

I can't deny that I must need a bath after four days in this bed. And I know he's already seen me naked—but like he said, I was unconscious for that. And I was high on pain meds. "I can do it myself. You don't have to be there. You don't have to…"

Watch. That's the word I almost said. He doesn't have to watch me bathe like a voyeur.

The unspoken word hangs in the air between us. His hard gaze challenges me. As does his hand reaching toward me. He grasps the blanket and pulls. A quick, efficient tug, and then I'm bared to the room. To his ice-blue eyes. To the disdain and desire he'll inevitably feel.

Of course I don't see any disdain. Or any desire. There's only clinical assessment in his cool gaze, methodically cataloguing every bruise and mark on my body. He looks every inch the doctor, even standing in a bedroom. The kind of doctor that attends the rich in their homes. It's hard to imagine this man murmuring words that sound of poetry. *Like the city at night. Beauty and danger.*

Cold air turns my nipples into hard peaks. I shiver in embarrassment. The clinical assessment seems somehow worse than sexual interest right now. I hate feeling weak, and there is no state weaker than being laid up in bed, almost an invalid.

"I can take a bath by myself," I say again, forcing false strength into my words.

One pale eyebrow raises. It calls me a liar.

"All right," he says, as calm as anything. He takes a step back, leaving the blanket out of my reach. There's only a bed with my naked body, a carpeted floor that might as well be a marathon, and an open door with the sound of water running. His body looks lean and impossibly strong as he crosses his arms and waits. And waits. And waits.

For the first time since he unveiled me I look down at myself, really examine my body, and what I find makes me blush. My legs are splayed like a baby doe who's never walked. I'm skinnier than I was a week ago, and it's not a good look on me, all ugly knobs. Even my breasts look smaller in the pale light of morning. God, no wonder he isn't attracted to me sexually.

I force myself to sit up. Dizziness swirls around me, and I clench my whole body not to heave. The idea of taking a bath even *with* help feels unlikely. My hair falls around my face, and I welcome the moment of privacy when I've been stripped bare—both physically and emotionally. Something tickles my neck, and I reach up to feel a tight row of something foreign. Stitches that go from my clavicle to my shoulder. Was that from when he knocked me down on the pavement? Or from when I fought him?

I remember again the glint in brown eyes, the certainty that he was going to kill me that night. I was supposed to hand over the chess piece. Instead I'd checked into that motel room empty handed.

In that moment I never thought I'd see another sunrise.

Keep going. One foot in front of the other. Part of me knew even as I lay there in that alley that my mother might already be dead. I can't accept that, though. I have to find out. Step one of that plan involves standing up and walking to the bathroom.

It takes every ounce of willpower to make myself do it. My body revolts at the very idea, fighting me with dead weight and sharp stabs of pain. It's like standing for the first time. My feet touch the floor. I try to remember how to straighten my legs.

Anders watches me without a hint of mercy in his pale blue eyes. He doesn't offer a hand to help me, and why would he? I insisted I could do this myself. I must look pathetic to him.

Then I'm standing.

For one second. Two. Dizziness swamps me again. The world tips over.

He catches me before I can even let out a cry. Strong arms scoop me up, and then the world twists again. I'm looking at the ceiling again, my arms wrapped around his neck, as if my body knows I can trust him even if my mind knows better. This close he's more sensation than man—the glint of sunlight off his blond hair, the starchy scent of his white shirt, the slight bow to his thin, hard lips.

A scent plays at my nose, something musky and complex and male. I don't even want to imagine what smells he's getting from me, when I haven't washed in days.

Steam envelopes me in the bathroom. It's already fogged up the mirrors and made the tile slick. An old-fashioned bathtub with claw feet and a freestanding faucet stands proudly in front of a bay window. Thin fabric blinds reveal trees and open sky. I've never seen a view like this in Tanglewood. We must be facing away from the city. Blue water swirls above white cotton towels. He's draped them along the sides and bottom of the tub.

He leans down, and my hands slide along his neck. I hold on tighter even as he lets me go. I sink into the hot water. A moan fills the humid air, long and low. I know as soon as I make the sound that it was wrong, that it was a mistake, that it sounds way too sexual, but I couldn't have held it in. Not when my body feels like it's found the spring of life. He only filled it to my waist. The water laps at my belly button like a sensual touch. The warmth seeps into my legs and hips, bone deep. The towels against the sides keep me from slipping. I rest my head back on a long sigh.

The planes of his face are harder now. He stands straight, about a million miles above me. It's how a climber would look once he's scaled a mountain. Strained. Proud. Possibly worried about the descent. The peak is only halfway there.

A small marble table holds soap. He picks it up in that same brusque, professional manner, except no doctor would do this, not even one paid to care for the rich. No ordinary doctor would lean down to wet the soap and slide it over my arm.

Anders isn't an ordinary doctor. He's my captor and my savior.

His hands are careful and gentle as he washes my arms, my shoulders. His palms rub over my breasts, soapy and callused, and I suck in a breath. Then he's moved away, but there's no relief from the tension, not when he's moving down—across my stomach, to my hips, my thighs. The scent of rose rises from the soap, and I have to fight to remember why it's a bad idea for him to touch me.

I'm a grown woman in a gorgeous bathroom, but I still feel like a little kid in a place with dark drains and cracked tile. My mother would crank our water heater up to full tilt to fill the bathtub. She would boil a pot of water on the stove and pour it in. Once a week I'd get those perfectly hot baths. It would be the pure luxury for a girl with too-short pants and a torn windbreaker. The only luxury we could afford, really. Even the hot dogs had to be rationed out between the noodles and beans.

"Where did you go?" a low voice murmurs.

I glance at Anders, who probably has no idea what it feels like be hungry or cold. How can he when a million-dollar chess piece is a family heirloom? "Memories."

"Bad ones," he says, rinsing the soap suds from my shoulder, his movements deft and careful as he avoids my stitches. "You look like someone kicked your puppy."

My step-father was supposed to change that for my mother. He was supposed to be a good man who went fishing on weekends and liked to watch sitcoms at night. He had a nice house. She would never be cold or hungry again, except she didn't know the dark side of him. She didn't know he would make me steal for him, wriggling my ten-year-old body through places too small for an adult to fit.

I close my eyes, blocking out the past. "Do you ever wonder if there was a moment, just a single moment where you made a decision that set you on this path? Do you ever wonder if you could have made a different decision, walked a different path?"

"Easy to blame yourself in hindsight. Much harder to predict the future."

I look at him, surprised by the understanding in his voice. He sounds sympathetic, which is ironic considering my path sent me to steal from him. "But you said there are moral absolutes."

"You might absolutely be on the wrong path. That doesn't mean you could have avoided it. The world can be a cold fucking place. It doesn't always give you a choice."

Those blue eyes challenge me at the same time as they sympathize with me. It's an invitation to tell him everything. A promise that he won't judge me too harshly. The temptation is as seductive as his fingertips stroking the inside of my elbows. I want to trust him, but there's nothing for me. It's an illusion, like the soapy water that shields me from his gaze—not really there. I can't give him back the chess piece, even if I had it in my pocket. It's the only thing keeping my mother safe. She never did see Victor for who he was. Not even now. I'm not sure how I'll get her out when she still doesn't believe that he's anything other than a doting husband. She's never trusted me, and that hurts the most. Sometimes I wonder why I'm fighting so freaking hard to protect someone who doesn't even believe me. But then I take a hot bath and remember how hard she worked to make my childhood bearable. There may be moral absolutes, but people are too complex to whittle down to *right* and *wrong*. Real people are messy. Even the man in front of me.

The warm water laps at my stomach, my hips, my arms. It lulls me into a sense of security. My eyes drift closed. "I can't remember the last time I had a bath."

"Only lukewarm showers in the motel room."

My throat constricts. I didn't want to steal on principle, but the truth is I didn't think it was harming anyone. Someone who owns a million-dollar chess piece isn't exactly struggling, are they?

Except I don't know anything about this man's struggles. The victim of my theft is no longer an abstract. He's flesh and blood. He's washing me.

"I'm sorry," I whisper. It's as close to a full confession as I can get.

Not even guilt can make me endanger my mother.

Two fingers under my chin. He lifts until I meet his gaze. "You didn't have a choice."

It's not a question. Anyone who saw my motel room knows I'm broke. My cheeks heat as I remember the door dented from some long-ago baseball bat, the mold climbing up the walls. He was in that room. He must have been to find me in the alley. "Don't make excuses for me."

"I don't have to. I see the way it's eating you up."

He doesn't bother to wait for an answer, not that I have one to give. Instead he moves to the foot of the bathtub. It's farther away and somehow more intimate, him looking at me head-on.

"Lift," he says, his voice gruffer than I remember. He pulls one foot from the water and soaps me there. Then the other one, his movements becoming slower, more languid. He still hasn't touched me between my legs. It's an omission that seems louder with every inch of skin he covers.

The rosewater has created a pink glow in the room. Or maybe that's my heat-tinged skin. Or maybe it's the desire that feels almost tangible in the space between us. I'm naked in front of a man who's wearing all his clothes. Only his sleeves are rolled up, the very edges stained dark from the splash.

He puts the soap back, and disappointment fills me.

Instead he picks up a small blush-colored tube that I'm guessing holds shampoo. Especially when he stands behind me, his hands pulling my hair away from my face. It clings to my skin from the sweat and the steam. His fingers are impossibly careful as he tucks the strands into the mass he's collected. These are the hands that stitched my wound and so avoided it when washing me. These are the hands of a healer.

"Lean forward." He definitely sounds deeper now, almost tearing off the words, fierce with them. A gold-plated stand holds a shower spray, and he sets the water to almost boiling. I make a squeak of pleasant protest before my scalp adjusts to the feel. He works the soap in his hands before running square-tipped fingers over my head. I have a brief thought that he's no longer in charge of me, he's serving me, and I don't know where the line between those two was. Then his fingers massage the shampoo into my scalp, and I can't think anymore. There's only bliss. Only this.

Time seems to lengthen and unroll as he moves the shampoo between every strand of hair. Even turning the spray back on to rinse doesn't lift the fog. He repeats the process with a creamy conditioner next, the moisture sliding between us in a way that's almost sexual. I catch him studying a strand of my hair, rubbing it between thumb and forefinger, bringing it to his nose to scent. His blue gaze meets mine, but he doesn't look abashed. If anything there's acknowledgment. Promise.

He takes his time rinsing the conditioner, letting the spray beat down on my shoulders, my neck, until I'm soft and malleable and burning hot. Everything feels completely right about this—being naked in front of him, being helpless beneath his hands. Being his. I know that if I looked down at his slacks I'd see the proof of his desire, but I can't look away from his eyes.

He shuts off the spray, and the sudden quiet in the room throbs with that one single part of my body he hasn't touched. It's a sultry melody, that knowledge. It bounces off the mirrors and the tiles. It floats on the dampness in the air.

The soap rests on the marble table, still slick from its earlier work.

He picks it up and looks at it. There's a war being fought inside him. A decision being made. He leans toward me, and my thighs part in anticipation. I'm ready for him, more than ready. I'm aching.

The soap is in front of me. He's holding it out, offering it to me. "You can wash there yourself," he says, but they're not words anymore. They're a rumble. They're a landslide.

I hold his gaze, which promises both pleasure and pain in equal portion. A smart woman would have avoided him altogether, but I'm here, I'm here. I'm already here, and if I'm going to have the pain, I deserve the pleasure, too. I grasp his wrist, and both of us freeze at the sensation. It's the first move I've made in this bathtub. No longer passive. Even this small action changes everything. I can feel the tendon and muscle and bone beneath my grip. And the warmth of him. God, he's burning.

"Please," I whisper. "Do it for me."

I'm talking about more than a bath. I'm talking about an orgasm and about protection. I'm talking about life, and the way I've been holding my head high through a million hard days. And this day, this one day, I want to let him do this for me.

"Yes," he breathes, the sound almost a groan.

He moves the bar of soap down my stomach, to the V between my legs. Even in this oversized bathtub there's not quite enough room to spread my thighs. That makes it feel more illicit when he wedges his way between them. He keeps the slick rectangle between us, using the corner to slide through my folds. My mouth opens on an intake of air. I'm frozen that way, clinging to the towel-covered curves of the tub, muscles taut. His hands still, his expression hard as he studies me.

Pale skin. Dark hair. Pink soap. The picture it makes is somehow pretty, almost wholesome until he angles his wrist. Smoothness touches my clit, and I let out a whimper.

"Go ahead." Lids hang low over winter-window eyes. "Take what you need."

The bar of soap hovers over my clit, not moving a bit. The lack of friction makes me ache. Tears prick my eyes. There's a yawning void inside me, and it won't only be filled by sexual release—but that's the only thing he's offering. "I can't."

"Want to see you move." The words could be a command. It's laced with a plea. He wants to see me move, and from the way his cheekbones have darkened, the way his arm muscles strain just to stay still, I think he *needs* to see me move. That need unlocks the box inside me. I'm not worried about how I look to him, whether I'm desperate or foolish. I can't give him the chess piece, but I can give him this.

I nudge my hips forward—only a centimeter. It feels like a hard, deep plunge into a sensual world. My clit slides against the bar of soap. Sensation sparks through my whole body. My breath chokes out, a halted sound echoing off the ceramic bathtub.

I'm panting as if I've run a mile.

Then I move again, rocking my hips.

My rhythm is jerky and uncertain. Water sloshes up the sides. The soap slides too low and too high and then right in the crevice that feels like home. The whole time his knuckles brush against me, scorching even against the backdrop of a hot bath. The whole thing is messy and wet and perfect.

"God," he mutters, watching me squirm. "You're perfect."

Not sexy. Not even beautiful. I'm perfect, as if he sees the real me. In this moment, with his crystal gaze searing my skin, it feels like he can see right to my very heart. To the heart that wants family more than anything, even my own innocence, even more than safety. I'll throw myself onto this icy fire to find it, and that's exactly what I've done, here I am.

His right hand holds the soap. His left cups the back of my neck. I let my head fall back. It bares my neck—a submissive pose. The evolutionary animal inside me recognizes that. His narrowed gaze and bared teeth prove he does, too. He bends down, and in a moment of wild thought, of relief, I think he's going to bite me. Mark me. Instead he places a feathersoft kiss above the stitches.

It's a match to a lifetime of kindling. Sorrow pours out of me from a thousand directions. Dry sobs wrack my body. The soap moves in a fatal slide, and climax clamps down on my body. That's how I peak—crying, coming, chanting his name. "Anders Anders Anders."

It seems to go on for eternity. It's over in a few blinding seconds.

The orgasm leaves my body as quickly as it arrived, leaving me slumped against the bathtub, every muscle drained and shaking, staring into blue-white eyes that blaze with male satisfaction.

He takes me out of the bathtub when my arms and legs are still made of jelly. His hands turn me this way and that, using a plush towel to dry me, as if I'm a doll he's taking care of. He's careful around each bruise and cut. This doll can feel pain. When I'm fully dry, he finds a tube of ointment and rubs white cream into each open abrasion. Steady hands lead me out of the bathroom. Part of me recognizes the thickness in his slacks. He needs something from me. Doesn't he? Except his hands don't feel needy as he guides me to the bed. Cool sheets. A soft pillow. Then sleep.

Chapter Nine

Anders

I follow the ambiguous scent of food to the kitchen, passing a dining room with china laid out as if it's a four-course meal instead of a random Tuesday dinner. I'm used to picking up an apple on my way through the Den's commercial kitchen or eating a power bar in my room.

One of the unintended side effects of keeping Natalie here is that I'm invited to sit down to dinner with Gabriel and Avery. I don't dislike it. I'm not sure I look forward to it, either.

Isolation comes too easily to me.

As I reach the doorway I smell something sharp and burnt. The kitchen is a whirlwind of chopped vegetables. Shards of carrots and celery and cabbage cover the countertop and sink—even the floor. A large pot gurgles on the stove. The bubbles are large and already at the rim.

The thing's about to spill over.

There are no people in sight, but I hear a small shuffling sound from the pantry. I look in, expecting to see Avery picking out ingredients. Instead there's a couple in the walk-in space, a man crowding a pregnant woman against the wall, his mouth on her neck, her eyes closed.

A small moan fills the space.

Shit. They're having a private moment. I start to back away. I'm soft on my feet, but Gabriel's damn near a predator. He whirls to face me, shielding her with his body.

"Hell," he says, his expression dark. Any man would be cross when interrupted this way.

"I'll come back later."

"No!" Avery says from over his shoulder. "Dinner's almost ready. Don't go away."

A low growl from Gabriel that I understand too well right now. It's pretty goddamn painful to have lust and nowhere to go. He curses under his breath but moves aside to let Avery run to the stove. Whatever's there has foamed and frothed, spilling into the shiny metal surface.

"Ohh no." She turns the range off and stirs gently until it calms down. "It looks okay, actually. I hope you like your noodles mushy and your chicken rubbery, though."

"I'm sure it will be delicious," Gabriel says, one golden eyebrow raised, daring me to disagree.

"Delicious," I say, because the last thing I'm going to do is complain about my dinner. Especially when cooked by a pregnant woman. I study the way she rests her hand on her back, the way her feet look swollen. I'm a doctor first, man second. Except when it comes to the woman upstairs. This woman looks tired and sore. "Are you sure you wouldn't rather use a meal delivery service?"

"No," Avery says vehemently, her hazel eyes flashing as she glances at me over her shoulder. "I have to figure this out. How am I going to feed a baby if I can't even make chicken noodle soup?"

I look at Gabriel, who shakes his head slightly. I'm missing the logic here, because you don't feed babies chicken noodle soup and I'm pretty sure Avery knows that. "Is this one of those hormone things?"

She gives me a venomous look, her hand stirring the pot so hard it looks like she wants to bash my head in with that wooden spoon. "No, it's a *mother* thing."

"She's worried," Gabriel says, his voice low.

"About the pregnancy? I can take her blood pressure again—"

"Not that. The mother thing. Being a good mother. Not turning out like hers."

Avery was an heiress at a blue-blood family in Tanglewood. Her mother was a socialite who died when she was young. Her father was a respected businessman—respected until he crossed Gabriel Miller. Then he was ruined, and the resulting desperation pushed Avery into his arms. "Abusive?" I ask, because I've seen too many terrible things to believe that all parents are good. Children with sunken eyes and repeated arm fractures. I was lucky. My parents were poor, but they loved me. They took care of me. Which makes it all the more important that I avenge them.

"Yes," he says. "Neglect anyway. She had a nanny to make sure she was fed and clothed and sent to school. The mom was too busy going to parties and having affairs to notice."

Ah. "So she thinks if she can cook…"

"Then she won't be the same. But she won't be the same no matter what. She isn't her mother, not in any shape or form. She'd throw herself in front of a bullet for this child. And she'd never step out on me."

"How do you know?"

A sharp look. "That a challenge, Anders?"

"Not really. I don't have a death wish." This man would tear the throat out of anyone who insulted his woman. "I don't think she'd step out either… but how do you *know*?"

"You're asking about trust."

Trust. A scary word when dealing with a woman who's already stolen from you. "I suppose so."

"There's no knowing, really. Otherwise it wouldn't be trust. There's only hoping."

"Hoping?"

This is a man whose business moves millions of dollars every day. He doesn't show his hand, but when he looks at Avery, there's no hiding the possessiveness in his golden gaze. "There's wanting it bad enough that it's harder to walk away than it is to take the risk."

Wanting it bad enough. It implies that trust is a choice. That love is a choice. The body and the heart can clamor all they want, but it's the mind that makes the decision to hope.

I help Gabriel and Avery carry large bowls of soup to the table. There's also rosemary pull-apart bread, mashed potatoes with gravy, and mac and cheese. It's like she looked up the words *comfort food* in a cookbook. And then made all of it. The bread's burnt on the bottom, the mashed potatoes are lumpy. The mac and cheese has solidified, but who the hell cares? A child raised in this home would know he was loved. Unlike Avery. And unlike, I'm beginning to suspect, the woman upstairs.

The soup has already begun to form a questionable oily surface across the top. "Looks great," I offer, because what the hell do I know? It looks fine. She doesn't need to worry.

She beams at me. "I hope you like it."

I take a bite of the chicken. It's… like rubber. *Chew.* And then swallow. "It's very… comforting."

That earns me a snort. "Listen, I'm glad you didn't get called out early. I wanted to talk to you about the woman upstairs. What did you say her name was?"

I didn't say what her name was, which I think she knows. "Natalie."

"Natalie." Her eyes narrow, and I have a glimpse of the heir to capitalist royalty. She may not know how to cook worth a damn but she could probably negotiate anything she wanted from hardened businessmen. I glance at Gabriel Miller, who's watching her with lazy approval. In a way, that's what she did. "How are her wounds? I saw her when you came in that first night."

"She's getting better." That's all I want to say, but her eyebrow raises and I know I won't be able to leave it at that. "Should be out of your hair in a couple days. Maybe sooner."

She frowns. "Does Natalie have somewhere safe to go?"

And that's the fucking problem, isn't it? Even if I find the chess piece, even if I get my revenge, what am I going to do with a woman? What am I going to do with a thief? With every day that passes, every hour, every second, it becomes more inconceivable that I would let her go.

"I'm working on it," I say, and then my phone vibrates on the table. I pick it up, seeing an address in the west side of Tanglewood, along with the letters *GSW*. Gun shot wound. "I've got to go. She's sleeping right now, but I'll leave a tray of dinner for her upstairs." I glance at the filmy soup. "If you can spare some. The door's locked. Don't interact with her."

"Christ," Gabriel says, and that's the only warning I have before Avery glares at me.

"She's not a prisoner, right?"

I stand, taking my plates that I've barely touched. These will work great for the tray I bring upstairs. "Of course she's not a prisoner." That's a lie. "But she's dangerous."

Gabriel shakes his head. "You have a lot to learn about women, my friend. You've just issued a challenge. Now I'm going to have the devil of a time keeping her from going in."

* * * *

Avery

The front door closes, and Gabriel's already out of his seat. He stalks across the dining room like a lion on the open plains. I'm his prey. "Wait," I say, backing up even as the dining chair stops me. "We have to finish dinner. Or at least clean up."

"Later." The word is a growl. He reaches me in a long, final stride. Strong hands lift me from the cushion as if I weigh nothing. He presses me against the wall. From far away it must look like he's manhandling me. Only I can feel how gentle his hands are as he caresses my shoulders, my arms, my hips. He's checking me over. It's something new that's started since I got pregnant, this ritual of confirming I'm still intact whenever we've been apart for more than two seconds.

I put my hands around his neck. "We can order delivery."

"Screw delivery. You're my dinner."

That makes me laugh. "You're silly when you're worked up."

He rewards that with a nip to my neck, and I gasp. "Christ, Avery. Christ."

I wouldn't have thought that pregnancy would be a sexy look on me. An aching back and swollen ankles aren't doing me any favors. I mean, sure, my nails have never been stronger—but that's not something they really feature in porn. Look how strong her nails are! Naturally shiny! But everything's been ramped up times a thousand since I started showing. Gabriel palms my breasts, and I know the larger size makes him crazy. He can't stop touching me there, can't stop holding them.

He bends down now, placing hot kisses across the plump curves and along the undersides. "Take that off if you want to keep it. I need you naked in the next three seconds."

An alarm rings in my head, because I know he isn't messing around. I pull the straps down my shoulders and push the stretchy material down. Cute maternity clothes are hard to come by, and I don't need him ripping another dress. He has the bra off before I can blink, and then he's choking out a groan, staring at me. Not my breasts, though. He's looking at my stomach, at the stretched skin and the belly button which decided to pop outward last week. "Look at you," he says, his voice low and almost menacing. Almost, if you didn't know him. Gabriel is hard and commanding and intensely physical. There's no holding him back from sex once he starts down that path. He's also caring and generous.

There is nothing he wouldn't do for our family.

My gaze flicks to the ceiling above us, where a young woman is locked in a room. "I think I should talk to her. What if she needs something that Anders doesn't know about?"

Gabriel's expression darkens. "No."

"I won't stay long. Or do anything to upset the baby."

"You heard him. She could be dangerous."

"Then why is she here? Why hasn't he called the cops if she's dangerous?" I'm not letting this go. His lips press together, because he knows I have a good point. "I think Anders is planning something else, and he's using her, maybe endangering her to do it."

"I should have told him no."

"To keeping a thief imprisoned in our second guest room? I mean, probably."

"He's done a lot for us." His gaze moves down, and I know he's thinking of the scare with my pregnancy early on. The bleeding and the way Anders had rushed to help me. It had been no big deal, but it felt terrifying. I have a regular doctor with the silhouette of a baby on the office door. We go there for regular checkups, but I know that Gabriel feels better with Anders watching over me.

He doesn't trust a lot of people in this world.

"He's done a lot for you," I say, knowing that Anders has patched up Gabriel more than once. I've seen it on a few horrifying occasions, and it probably happened even more. My husband wears a suit to work every day, but he doesn't always do his work over a shining boardroom table. His past is darker than that. Messier. And I love him, which means accepting every part of that.

A kiss at the corner of my lips. On my nose. On my chin. "Do you trust me?"

Ugh. "Don't play that card."

"Do you trust me?"

"Of course I do."

"Then trust me that Anders is trying to protect that woman upstairs. And so am I. You saw the condition she came here in.

Someone left her to die. They'd be back for round two if they know she's alive."

My hands tighten on him. "Then why doesn't he call the cops?"

"I'm not sure exactly. I don't have all the details. I don't think he does either, but if I had to guess, I'd say that the person who did this is a cop. Or at least connected with law enforcement."

My eyes close. "All this for a chess piece."

It's not that I don't understand the value of chess. Its importance to intellectual and cultural history is unparalleled. This house is filled with rare boards and pieces that Gabriel has gifted me. It's the irony that gets me. A game about war. As if there's anything playful about violence. I remember the blood and bruises on that young woman as Anders carried her upstairs. As if her life is a piece to be sacrificed.

Gabriel puts his forehead to mine. "Don't worry about her."

I'm worried about her because no one else seems to be. I believe that Gabriel and Anders don't want her hurt. That doesn't mean they'll manage to keep her safe. Pawns have a way of getting caught in the crossfire. That's something I learned firsthand. I pull him down for a kiss. "Distract me," I say, but I'm not really telling the truth. It's not me who needs a distraction. It's him, the man I love.

Chapter Ten

Natalie

A tray of barely edible food waits for me when I wake up.

After swallowing a few bites using the bedsheet as a cape, I explore the room. There's a little basket of temporary toiletries in the bathroom—disposable toothbrushes and tiny tubes of toothpaste. This is clearly someone's carefully stocked guest room, but the lock on that door is not an ordinary one. Whoever owns this house is both a great host and also kind of scary. One of the dresser drawers contains a small stack of women's clothes. I pull on jeans and a T-shirt. No bra or panties, and I wonder whether that's a deliberate omission on Anders' part or just male cluelessness. A soft knock at the door makes me whirl.

"Anders." His name forms on my lips, but the person who opens the door isn't a six-foot Nordic god with uncompromising blue eyes and an uncanny ability to see through me. It's a woman.

"Hi," she says with an uncertain smile. "I know this is strange, but I wanted to check on you. Do you need anything? Something else to eat? I know the soup is terrible. We can UberEats something."

I stare at her, wondering if this is another dream. I've been having strange ones. I don't know whether it's the lingering effects of the attack or the foreign feeling of this super-luxury bed, but I've been having nightmares about chess boards that go on forever. "No, I'm... I'm fine. I had some of the soup. It was good."

She rolls her eyes, but I think she looks pleased. "I know it's bad, but I'm trying. I figure as long as I keep trying… that's the important part, right? Listen, I don't want to insult you, but you aren't dangerous, are you? You aren't going to hurt me?"

I glance down at her stomach, which is large and round. This is who I've become. A thief. A criminal. Someone a pregnant woman has to worry about. My stomach falls a thousand feet and lands with a thud. "No. Honestly. God, I… I swear on everything I care about that I'd never hurt you. Or anyone. I know you have no reason to believe me but—"

She waves off my words as she sails into the room. "I didn't think so."

The door hangs open an inch, and I have a brief thought about running. I'm not sure what kind of security this place has, but there'll never be a clearer exit route than this. Which makes me face the fact that I'm less of a prisoner here and more of a guest. I don't *want* to leave.

Especially without seeing Anders again.

The woman's already on the bed, leaning back against the headboard, a look of relief on her pretty face. "I hope you don't mind me being on the bed, but I need to sit."

"Of course I don't mind. I mean, it's your bed."

"Look, we're not in the habit of keeping people locked up here."

Cautiously I sit down cross legged on the bed with her. "I didn't think you were."

"But I figured you couldn't be too dangerous, because I don't think Gabriel would have let you stay. He has a soft spot for people in trouble, even though he'd hate for me to say that. Are you in trouble?"

She's very straightforward, which is comforting. I'd rather know where I stand with someone. She also reminds me of the girl in class with gorgeous curls in her hair and expensive clothes. The kind of person I was never cool enough to be friends with. But she isn't looking at me with judgment. Instead she looks curious.

"So much trouble," I whisper. The truth slides out of me, as slippery as that pink soap in the bath earlier, provocative and smooth and alluring when it has no right to be.

"Anders will help you." Her voice has complete confidence. Somehow, I find myself believing her. Maybe that's only because I want to. It occurs to me that she's the best source of information about Anders that I'll find. After all, he brought me here, not where he lives.

"Have you known him long?"

"Does anyone really know him?" She makes a face. "He's so stoic all the time. But I suppose we know him best. Me and Gabriel. And Damon Scott, at the Den."

The Den, where I stole the chess piece. Acid rises in my throat. The rubbery chicken threatens to come back up. I force myself to breathe steadily. "I know he wants the bishop back."

"It's not the piece he wants. It's the person who stole it."

Surely she knows… "That's me."

One eyebrow raises. "Do you know *why* this chess piece is so valuable? What's the provenance? What's the significance? Do you know anything about it that wasn't written on that tiny placard?"

I shift on the bed uneasily. "Not really."

"Exactly." She looks satisfied. "Someone had you steal it. Someone who knows about chess. Someone who cares about its history. That's the person who Anders is looking for. And if I had to guess, that's the person who gave you those bruises."

My stomach tightens. "What I don't understand is why. It's almost like Anders is more interested in the person who wants the chess piece than the money it would have gotten. Why?"

Hazel eyes turn solemn. "You'll have to ask him that."

Chapter Eleven

Anders

I smell like disinfectant and sweat. My body knows that, but my mind keeps reliving the metallic scent of blood. Such a small piece of metal can do untold damage to human flesh. The man survived, but it will be touch and go for a few days. I patched him up so that he can live another day, fight another day—and maybe in a few months put a bullet in another person that I'll have to sew up.

It's hard not to feel jaded sometimes. A spiral staircase leads to the conservatory which has a hundred windows. It makes me feel like I'm part of the stars. That helps a little bit. Not as much as seeing Natalie would help. I'd like to give her a bath and fuck her with the bar of soap again, but it's late. She's probably asleep. She needs her rest. I have a thousand other arguments that I should leave her alone.

"Anders?"

I turn and see her at the top of the staircase, only her head and shoulders visible from the room. It's almost like my thoughts conjured her. "How did you get out?"

If I showed emotion at all, I would wince at the harsh tone of voice. I'm actually happy to see her. So naturally, the first thing I do is make her feel unwelcome.

Even in the pale light I can see her cheeks darken. "Avery came to visit me. Don't be mad at her. She was just worried about me. I promised her you were treating me okay."

"Hell." I run a hand over my face. "Gabriel's going to lose his shit."

She makes a face. "Because I could have hurt her."

Her tone of voice is cavalier, but I see the pain in her eyes. God, she's vulnerable. So tough on the outside. Soft on the inside. It would be so easy to push her away, so easy to damage her that it makes me angry at the world. "You wouldn't hurt a goddamn fly."

That small chin lifts in defiance. "How would you know? I'm already a thief. Maybe I'm a murderer, too."

"Do you know that bullets actually sear the skin? Cook it hard and fast until it's as black as the bottom of that bread Avery made tonight. The first thing I have to do, before I can even pull out the metal, is cut away the burnt skin. Slice it off like it's the part of a steak you don't want to eat."

She flinches. "Oh, Anders. I'm sorry."

Does she see how jaded I am? "It doesn't bother me anymore. But it clearly bothers you. You aren't a murderer. I took care of you for days while you were drugged and in and out of sleep. You get to know a person that way."

Tears fill her eyes. "Is that where you were tonight? Avery said you got a call."

I turn toward the stars. "You should go to sleep."

A soft touch on my arm. "You're the one who needs rest. I'm not sure when you get the time. You're taking care of strangers like the whole weight of the city rests on your shoulders."

"Are you going to try and psychoanalyze me?" A coarse laugh. "I should warn you it might take a few years to get through this rat's nest inside my head. And it won't be pretty."

Her voice floats in the darkness. "I'm not trying to psychoanalyze you. But I'm here if you want to talk. Or close your eyes for a few minutes. You deserve a moment of peace."

I give her a sharp glance, trying to ignore how beautiful her face looks gilded in moonlight, how ephemeral she seems in the shadows. "What if I tell you finding the bishop will bring me peace?"

A rueful smile. "Then I'd say you were lying."

Christ. I hate that she's right. She may not be trying to psychoanalyze me, but she's somehow managed to hit upon the truth. Nothing about my revenge mission makes me feel calm. Only furious. It could be that taking care of someone like that is an intimacy that goes both ways. While she was half-conscious she was collecting information about me; she knows me as well as I know her.

Dark eyes search mine. There's urgency and concern. "You don't want the piece back, really. You want the person who… you want the person who told me to get it. Why?"

"Doesn't matter. What matters is that I find them."

"How do you know it's not me? I could have wanted the chess piece for myself."

"Not likely." I give her a glance, acknowledging the last time we stood side by side. We were in the Den, looking at a painting then. Now we're standing in front of the sky. Both of them dark, both mysterious. Both beautiful. "You haven't spared a single glance at the chess set on the table. It's worth a small fortune. A birthday present from Gabriel to Avery."

She glances back at the unassuming set of carved ivory pieces. "That one?" Her tone is doubtful.

"A collector would know that it comes from India in the 1700s. A historian might know that it was owned by Phillip Stamma, the man who invented notation. He's carved them right onto the board. Whereas you're far more interested in that painting over there."

There's art tucked into a few different pockets of the room, even some stained glass framed in the window, but she knows immediately which piece I'm talking about. "It's not a print, is it? That's a real Harper St. Claire. Look at the eyes. You can see it."

"Avery's friends with her."

Her mouth drops open, which shouldn't look so adorable. My hardened criminal is awe-struck at the idea of knowing a contemporary painter. Would she be equally impressed if I told her that I'd actually gone to a Christmas party at the penthouse apartment Harper St. Claire shares with her fiancé? She'd given me a white metal lunchbox with the words *Human Organ for Transplant* in red block letters.

She steps closer to examine the painting, which features a Valkyrie in full headdress and armor carrying a pile of textbooks as she closes her locker in a typical high school hallway. It's more of a sketch, not the large-scale statement paintings she's known for. Only a true fan would recognize the artist.

In fact it's possible even a true fan wouldn't recognize it. I cock my head, considering the young woman standing in front of me. It's hard for me to reconcile the different pieces of her. The sexy temptress from the Den. The stealthy criminal who penetrated Damon's defenses. The vulnerable young woman in front of me, more excited by something torn out of a sketchbook than by a thirty-thousand-dollar chess set.

"You're an artist," I say slowly. "The artist. N. Lhuirs. That's you."

She doesn't move. I can't see her face from where I stand, but I can picture the surprise, maybe even the embarrassment of being caught. The fear.

I grasp her wrist gently and turn her to face me. There's the fear I didn't want to see. Maybe a hint of pride. That more than anything makes the blood pump heavily in my veins. A million different facets of one woman, like a diamond turning in the dark. This is the one that makes me hard—the artist who wants to paint more than anything else.

"Does it really matter?"

"That's how you got into the preview party. You weren't on the invite list. No one could tell me your name, like you were goddamn Cinderella. Only the valet remembered someone showing up in a cab, strange because no one takes a yellow car if they can take their Bentley."

She looks down, but I tilt her head up. I want those dark eyes. I want those black swaths of paint overlaid with gold. They're shimmering with tears. "I said it would never work, submitting my paintings for the auction. What do a bunch of rich people want with my work? But they said they'd consider them, and Damon Scott approved them to be included. And I kept thinking, why couldn't this be real? Why couldn't I really sell my paintings instead of doing it just to steal?"

Fear shines as strong as the stars above us. "What did he do to you?"

The night holds its breath while she looks at me. Darkness and light collide. There's a trust so deep between us that it feels strange that I ever doubted it, that I asked Gabriel about it. It's as real as the floor beneath my feet. As real as the soft touch of her skin. A dark lock of her hair falls across her olive-toned forehead. I move to brush it away, and she flinches—as if I were going to hit her.

It's an alarm bell clanging. It shatters the moment, the trust. Whatever she might have been about to tell me evaporates into the night. She looks sideways at the chess set. "Do you play?"

"Yes."

"I never learned. It was strictly checkers for me. Maybe a little tic tac toe."

"Do you want to learn?"

"The truth is I'm not really book smart. I always feel better when I have a paintbrush in my hand." She gives a small laugh. "Still life.

Portraits. I'll do it all, but I like abstract stuff the best. You were right when you said I was one of those. Who thinks art can mean anything."

"My mother lost the ability to read, but she could still play."

There's curiosity in her expression, but she doesn't ask. "Can you show me?"

A small wrought-iron table holds the wooden board. Two matching chairs are on opposite sides. I pull out one of the chairs for Natalie, glad that she'll be sitting. She should really be resting, but I don't have the heart to make her go back to bed. I'm too selfish to send her away. "The pawns," I say, pointing to the row of small pieces forming the front row. "They can only move forward. Mostly one step. Two, if it's the first time it's moved."

She taps the tallest piece. "This one's the king. I know their names, but that's about it."

I pick up the bishop, which in this set is a rather plain dome. "He wasn't always a bishop. He started as an elephant, like one you'd use in battle. In France he became a jester. In Italy, the one who holds the flag. Those two prongs at the top meant different things to every culture."

"So many different sides of one piece."

Different sides? Strange. I always thought of him being replaced in each culture. A new piece, instead of the same one being shown in different lights. It reminds me of the woman sitting in front of me, the different facets that form the single gemstone.

"In the European feudal structure he became a bishop. And the piece you took? That was the very first one in recorded history. It was found on a hill in what's now Scotland."

"The first one?"

"There's some dispute about which country created him. Naturally Scotland wants credit, but there's some evidence it came over from Norway. Ireland makes some noise about it. Then again, the map looked a little different in medieval times."

"How did your family come to have it?"

"It was my mother's. She came from a family with money, but she never wanted dresses or diamonds. This was what they got her instead. Ancient chess pieces and a doctor's degree. Trinkets, really, for a spoiled heiress. They were shocked when she actually wanted to practice medicine. The bishops were the only thing she took when she left home."

"Bishops?" Her eyes go wide.

Of course she'd notice that slip. Then again, her surprise does look genuine. Who the hell is pulling the strings here? "Yes, there were two. A perfect pair."

She picks up the bishop opposite mine. Her thumb rubs over the dull wood grain in almost a caress. I feel it acutely over my own skin. Heat. Desire. I don't want to play chess with her. I don't want to *think* right now. I want to feel.

"Natalie," I say, and my voice has dropped an octave.

Her gaze meets mine, and the spark in her dark eyes shows she recognizes my tone. The way her body shifts shows she isn't immune. Her finger rubs over the piece again—that small point of her finger running along smooth carved wood. "Yes?"

"Take me to bed."

"Is that a request or an order?"

"I'm damn near begging."

She looks away, and I can feel her longing like a physical pull. "Is this for the bishop? Or whatever you're after with this auction? Like payment since you didn't get the money?"

Hell. There are only a few loops of iron between us, a few feet of wood, but it's too much. I shove the whole table aside. The screen resounds in the small space. Then I'm dragging her into my arms. This close I can smell more than antiseptic and memory. This close I can smell arousal. "This is because I want you. And because you want me. Fuck anything else."

Doubt darkens her gaze. I realize it's not me who's the barrier to trust in this relationship. It's her and the demons who haunt her. I had parents who loved each other. Our family was full of pain, but it had laughter, too. Feeling her worry, her pain makes me want to punch something. Someone. Whoever it is that made her steal the chess piece.

Was he her lover? Her brother? Either way, he hurt her. Made her do *this* instead of painting.

Which means she's mine now.

I'm going to make sure she attends the next auction as a featured guest, instead of sneaking through security on a loophole. I'm going to make sure Damon makes a whole goddamn showcase for her work.

Later.

Right now I lead her downstairs to her room. I shut the door behind us, because I need to lose myself in her soft skin and sweet understanding. I need to lose myself in the salt of her body.

Chapter Twelve

Natalie

The conservatory held a kind of magic, as if anything were possible—as if he and I were equals without impossible barriers between us. Once I follow him down to my room, everything changes. Reality's waiting for me, in the form of his searching gaze and doctor's hands reaching for my chin. He wants to *examine* me, and after days of feeling sick, I'm tired of it.

I bat his hand away. "I'm fine."

A raised blond eyebrow calls me a liar. "You don't want me to touch you?"

"No," I say, reveling in the power he gives me. "I want to touch *you.*"

He pauses, and I have the sense that he wants to tell me no. He wants the control. Deliberation. Weighing. He's judging the value of my demand as surely as those patrons examined the pieces for auction. Finally he opens his hands. "Then touch me."

It's not precisely inviting, the way he stands there watching me—almost daring me to change my mind. Not precisely inviting the way he's fully clothed. Maybe if I were still on campus, worried about my latest piece or my grades, I might have lost the nerve. This is another world. Another planet. I'm on Mars, where women steal priceless chess pieces and men capture them for it.

In this foreign place I can take what I need.

I place my hands on his chest, first, flush against his crisp shirt. There's a faint scent coming from it—antiseptic or something medicinal. It's a reminder of the violence he saw tonight. A reminder of what he is: a healer, first and foremost. That healer's heart beats steady beneath my hands.

Deep breath. I undo a single button. Then another.

Soon a white undershirt is the only thing keeping his chest from my sight.

I pull up the dress shirt along with it—except he's way too tall. I stand there awkwardly, holding it up, not nearly close enough to get it over his head. After a pause, almost as if he wants to emphasize the difference in our sizes, he takes it off himself.

His chest is broad and scarred like a warrior. I trace the line of muscles across his shoulder and over his pecs. My finger brushes the flat of his nipple, and his abs tense. Those rigid lines draw my attention, and I walk two fingers down the ladder. "You're strong," I say, feeling almost sad about it. He's beautiful, like a caged white tiger in a zoo. "It's because of the chess piece, isn't it? Because of who you're looking for? That's why you keep in such good shape."

He lifts one shoulder. "The places I practice medicine, they aren't clinics on the upper east side. I don't work in shiny hospitals where everyone has insurance."

In other words, even his work is dangerous.

"Tan," I say, touching the burnished skin along his arm. "And white." The place where his waist tapers is pale, not exposed to the sun. Blond hairs on his stomach point down, where dress pants block my view. *Be brave, Natalie. You started this.* I undo his pants with shaking hands.

His own hands twitch at his sides, as if he's struggling to let me do it. I don't think this man cedes control very often. The idea lends me strength—this is hard for me, but it's hard for him, too.

And then his pants are off. His briefs go with them.

I'm looking at a cock so engorged it looks like pain. The bulbous head is reddish, flushed with arousal, the tip glistening. "I'd paint you white and beige," I whisper, my gaze flicking to his icy eyes. "And blue, of course. Then there'd be these faint streaks of red, almost hard to pick out, hard to identify, but *there*, part of you, anger and violence and passion."

His cock jumps at the last word, and I suck in a breath. "Natalie," he says, his voice low like it was in the conservatory.

"Yes?" I say, remembering the way he watched me touch the bishop, the way I stroked my finger over the ridges to tease him. I'm not powerless here.

"I'm going to take you now. Tell me no before it's too late."

No? I run my finger down his abs, over the flat beneath them, until they touch the pale fur at his groin. Then I stroke his cock—still using only a single finger—more a tease than an attempt to pleasure. "Too late for what?"

The tendons in his neck stand out. "I'm not going to be gentle. You have to understand, whatever you think about me, I'm not gentle. I'm not going to take you soft. The way I feel about you now, I'm putting my cock inside you, and I'm not leaving until I've come two, three—no, not until I've come four times."

My breathing quickens, and I feel a clench between my legs. It shouldn't be so appealing, the idea of being taken without regard for my own pleasure. "What if it hurts?"

He throws his head back, baring his teeth. "Of course it's going to hurt. You're small and weakened from your attack, and I'm a goddamn rutting animal. It will tear you apart."

A squeeze, hard, deep inside my sex. "Please."

Am I begging him to stop? Or to start? I don't know anymore. He doesn't either. "Hell."

A goddamn rutting animal. Maybe that's what all of us are, when it comes to something as primal as sex. It doesn't matter what I saw when we're both reduced to our core beings. I lean forward and press my nose against his chest, breathing in the Anders scent, feeling his chest hair tickle my nose.

And then, very carefully, I bite his muscle.

An intake of breath. A growl, unmistakable, that sends shivers up my spine.

Then he's on me, surrounding me, pressing me up against a wall. Something clatters to the ground. Something crashes. The air's knocked out of me, and then I'm full—so full it *hurts*. There's a tear, a burn. I make a sound of anxious desire in my throat. He presses his whole body against me, that place rubbing against my clit, making everything bearable and rose-hued and light.

My mouth falls open, and I rock my hips in helpless request.

He gives me what I need—a single thrust, hard enough to obliterate all thought from my head. The chess piece doesn't exist. The fading bruises never happened. Nothing matters except the wedge of hot male flesh inside my body. I look down and realize with dazed surprise that I'm almost fully dressed, wearing only a loose sundress. It's a stark contrast to the muscled nakedness of this man. A stark contrast to the last time he touched me, wearing a dress shirt and slacks while I was in the bath.

There's something wild about being dressed like this when he fucks me, when he shoves himself inside me, as if he's an ancient Nordic warrior, a Viking come to plunder me.

He moves faster and faster. It's all I can do to cling to his broad shoulders.

"I need—I need—"

"I know what you need," he says, his eyes blazing with certainty.

And then he's pushing me up some invisible hill, almost dragging me against my will toward orgasm. I don't know why I would fight it, except that it's too fast, and this is too hard, and I'm spinning out of control with his body holding me open, unable to do anything but surrender. He shifts the angle, fucking upward, and his cock touches some place inside me that feels like a live wire. I scream as the climax blinds me, and he roars as his cock pulses inside me, claiming me but also giving in, spilling his seed in a messy, slick slide.

I pant against his shoulder, my mouth open, tears of shock slipping down my cheeks.

"You okay?" he asks gruffly, brushing a tear with his thumb.

"Yes. Just. A lot." I pant the words, but he seems to make sense of them.

He leans forward to lick a tear from my cheek. Then he moves us both to the bed without dislodging himself. I'm lying down with him between my legs. He pulls away gently and then pushes back in. The oversensitive flesh screams in protest. "Wait," I say, laughing or sobbing. "Wait. Wait."

A slow shake of his head. Those blue eyes are merciless. "No waiting."

"It's too fast. We just—"

"I gave you fair warning, little thief. I'm not leaving this sweet body until I've come three more times."

* * * *

Natalie

I wake to the feeling of complete warmth, the kind that seeps all the way into the center of my body, the kind I've really only dreamed about. This would feel like a dream, too, except that I have to pee. My body fights me every step of the way. It wants to stay on this warm, muscled, steadily breathing pillow forever. Instead I slip out of bed and go to the bathroom. When I wash my hands I catch sight of myself in the mirror. Wild hair in a thousand knots. Bruises that look mottled-yellow in my skin. I look like a mess, except for my eyes. Those look strangely content. That might have been the only full night's sleep I've ever had. No going out at dusk to do something for my step-father. No waking up at 3 am with my breath coming fast, fear in my throat.

When I enter the bedroom, I'm greeted by a drowsy blue gaze. "Come here," Anders says.

Intimacy in the dark means one thing. Cuddling the morning after means something else. I'm not in a place where I can be in a relationship. And definitely not with this man. I find myself climbing in anyway. He pulls me close, my back to his chest, his heavy arm wrapped around me, his face in my hair. He doesn't seem to mind that it's a bird's nest back there. He breathes in deep.

"My dad died when I was five."

He makes a small sound—sympathy? Regret? I'm ruining the moment with my confession, but after watching him take care of me, after seeing him tend to my wounds and my body, even when he has every right to hate me, I owe him this. Now. When it's hardest.

"I don't really remember him. It was my mom and me for most of my childhood. We didn't have much, you know? She'd always look through magazines, dreaming out loud what it would be like when we could buy a marble table or a grand piano. Or a car that doesn't have someone else's cigarette burns. But it didn't feel like a bad life. We had each other. It was us against the world."

His arm tightens around me. I feel his erection pressing against my ass, but he doesn't push it against me. He does nothing but hold me. "What changed?"

"She dated a lot. A lot of losers, really. I'd wake up and walk out in my Little Mermaid pajamas looking for cereal, and there'd be some stranger watching TV on the couch with no shirt on."

He tenses. "They ever put their hands on you?"

I try to keep my voice light. "She probably dated every asshole in the city limits, so yeah, statistically, a few of them were bound to be a creep. I learned to manage them."

"Their names."

My laugh sounds forced. "What are you going to do? Track them down?"

His silence answers the question.

"Well, it doesn't matter. It was a long time ago." Besides, that wasn't the worst part. "Then she met this guy, and he seemed so... normal. He liked chicken fried steak and romantic movies. We even started going to church every Sunday because it was important to him. I was the flower girl when they got married. I thought... I thought we could be a family."

"Hell," he says, clearly not liking where this story's going.

"He started hitting her a few months later. Maybe it was sooner, I don't know. That was when I found out. I thought that would be the worst, you know? What could be worse than that? Except he told me there was a way I could keep her safe. If I did one little favor. All I had to do was borrow someone's phone when we were in church—borrow it for fifteen minutes and then put it back, without him noticing. And he wouldn't hit my mother."

"I'm going to kill him."

"Don't," I say, panic rising in my chest. "Don't. He has friends, okay? And it's not that simple."

"What's not simple about it?"

"He's a cop."

He turns me so I'm facing him. Propped up on one elbow, the morning sun highlighting his muscled chest, he looks impossibly handsome. A fairy tale prince that I don't deserve. "This is why you didn't want to go to the hospital. You knew he could find you there."

I look down, studying the pattern of blond hair on his chest. "He doesn't usually hit me, but I didn't do what he wanted. I started realizing... it was never going to stop. There would always be one more favor. Always one more threat. So I stole the chess piece, but I didn't give it to him."

"It's your insurance policy."

I search his blue gaze for understanding. "I just had to do

something. Had to fight back."

"Of course you did." He presses a soft kiss to my forehead. "But you don't have to fight alone. Not anymore. Tell me where it is, Natalie. Let me help you."

Is that real? I don't have to fight by myself? "This is my problem to solve."

"Hell. You said it looked like I held the weight of the whole city on my shoulders. You're doing the same thing. It's not your responsibility to fight this by yourself."

The allure is almost enough to level me. I want the comfort he's offering me. The friendship. More than friendship if his stroking fingers on my thigh are any indication. Except I can't let him get involved in this. I wasn't kidding—Norman has friends in the department. People who will protect him, who will avenge him. When I stand against him, I have to stand alone.

"I can't," I whisper.

He doesn't look surprised. Only disappointed. He turns me again, and I brace myself for rejection. For him to leave the bed or maybe kick me out. Except he pulls me close.

Chapter Thirteen

Anders

I stamp my feet on the ground, but cold air still seeps into my legs. Pine needles prick through the fabric. Freezing drops of water fall intermittently from the treetops. Give me inner city apartments and dark alleyways any day. This nature shit isn't for me.

My phone buzzes. I read a message from my investigator. *Natalie Lhuirs, age 24. Graduate student enrolled at the University of Illinois, School of Art + Design.*

I'm already typing back an answer. *You find the accomplice?*

A little bubble appears with three dots. Then, *Roommate says she goes to school all day, works in the evenings. She visits home every few months — in Tanglewood.*

Where's her family?

No word yet. There are 2K Lhuirs in the Tanglewood city limits. More if you include surrounding areas. That's assuming she's got the same last name. I'll have more in a few hours.

In a few hours it might be too late.

Her stitches mostly dissolved. Her bruises mostly healed. She's back to fighting form, and a conveniently fake call on my cell phone about an emergency provides her with the perfect opportunity to escape.

I have a clear view of the house. In particular, I have a clear view of the second story on the right-hand side. That's where I can see my very own Disney princess rappelling down the brick wall. She's not using long hair. Instead she has what's probably twelve thousand thread count sheets tied into a rope.

For a few, cold, miserable minutes out here in the dark I thought she wasn't going to take the bait. Her slender figure moves quickly over the hill. She almost blends in with the night. If this is how she looked near the Den, it's no wonder she managed to breach their defenses. They're prepared for an assault. She's practically invisible. Only when she rounds the building do I step out of the trees. Someone steps with me. A tall silhouette. "Hell," I say.

Gabriel shakes his head, looking a bit like a wild animal getting the water out of his fur. "That took forever, didn't it? Thought she was actually going to sleep for a minute there."

"What the hell are you doing here?"

"Same thing you're doing. Following her so we can find out who's pulling the strings."

I turn up the collar on my coat and stuff my hands into my pocket. It's going to be a long, miserable walk tailing this woman. "You should go back to Avery. She probably needs a foot rub or something."

"Nah, I'll do it when I get back. Otherwise you're going to get lost."

We round the building, following in Natalie's footsteps. Only to see red taillights wink in the distance. "Fuck," I say, striding to my car. "Where did she find a ride?"

Gabriel slings himself into the passenger seat. "Uber for criminals?"

I ignore him as we drive without headlights. Lucky for me Gabriel lives out in the land of rolling, expansive estates. Meaning there aren't a lot of cars. And there are even fewer Honda Civics. We follow it from a safe distance. The car in front rounds a bend. When I reach the same place, there's a T in the road. No sign of those red tail lights.

"Turn right," Gabriel says.

"How do you know?" I say, but I'm already following his directions.

"It's the only way out of the neighborhood. Aren't you glad you brought me along now?"

"Thanks," I say, and I know I sound surly, but I don't like the idea of using Natalie as bait. It feels too uncomfortably close to the way she's been used before. Except my goal isn't to harm her. No, I want to protect her. The only way I can do that is by finding out who's behind this.

It's only a fringe benefit that I'll also find out who hurt my mother.

Tracking becomes easier when we hit the highway. There are more cars around. Less chance they'll recognize someone tailing them. I stay a few cars behind. Part of me wants to keep my focus on the mission. Find out who's pulling the strings, as Gabriel put it. And eliminate the threat. The other part of me, the *doctor* part of me, can't help cataloging all the things that can go wrong. The human body is so fucking fragile. And none more than the woman in that 1998 navy blue sedan.

We hit the west side, which isn't exactly a surprise. There's plenty of criminal activity here. There's also the Den, right in the very heart. That's where the sedan slows down. Natalie hops out of the car before it's even fully stopped, and then it zooms away. She pauses a moment to look up at the Den. The third floor. That's where I keep my room, though it's a cold and lonely place. Sterile, really. Then she walks right through the front door.

"What?" I say, fury rising inside me.

"Absolutely not." Gabriel's already shaking his head. "No way Damon had anything to do with this."

He might have. He could have wanted the full auction price for the chess piece, arranged its disappearance, and kept the money. It would have been so fucking easy in his own building. The guilt and the offer of repayment—all of it could have been a show. "Then why's she waltzing in like she has any business being there?"

"I don't know, but I trust him like I trust you. With my life."

That makes me pause. There are a lot of people who trust their lives to me. It comes with the medical degree. All of them are strangers. Even my father withdrew so far after my mother died that he was like a stranger to me. There are only a few people in the world who know me. Gabriel is one of them. Damon is another. Friendship. I would have admitted the term reluctantly, but it's more than that, I realize now. It's family. That's why I keep a room in the Den. Not because it's conveniently located for midnight emergency calls in the west side. Because Damon and Penny are family. So are Gabriel and Avery. And the little wriggly potato inside her stomach.

A car pulls up in front of the Den.

A dark blue Taurus.

Anyone could identify it as a law enforcement officer a mile away.

I tense, because this might be Natalie's step-father.

Except when a woman emerges from the car, wearing a buttoned-up gray suit, and a man who might be younger than her comes out of the passenger side, one thing is clear: these are feds. It's puzzling, because I know Damon Scott would never call them in. Someone could steal the crown jewels out of his pocket, and he'd handle it personally.

Unless someone else called them.

The pieces fall into place with horrifying solidity. Natalie going into the Den, the scene of her crime. The feds, who should have no business here. The problem of the corrupt cops.

This is my problem to solve. She's going to turn herself in.

I'm across the street in a flash, a second behind the feds through the door. I glare at the bouncer, who gives me a shrug, as if to say, "Feds. What are you going to do?" Except he doesn't do shit without Damon's approval. He might not have set this whole theft up, but would he be willing to accept the feds to get it solved? Maybe. Especially if it was Natalie's condition. *Bring in the feds, and I'll give you the bishop.* She doesn't think she knows how to play chess, but she does. She's sacrificing a pawn—herself.

I meet the feds in the foyer, who are standing around looking stern and fucking useless.

"Excuse me," I say, pushing past them. If I can find Natalie before it's too late... Then Damon appears outside his office, and I know it's over. He looks resigned but also satisfied. It's the look of a man who's about to have his auction business in the green.

Natalie appears behind him, her expression determined. Her eyes widen when she sees me, but she doesn't say a word. Doesn't run to my side. Doesn't *trust* me to solve this for her.

Damon walks to the ballroom and presses his thumb to the scanner. "It really was a puzzle for me, how anyone made it inside with the fancy tech system we've got around this room."

"Cameras?" the lady fed asks.

Damon snorts. "So you can subpoena them to use against my patrons? No, thank you. But there *are* logs of who comes in and out of this room. No one entered the room before me that day."

"It doesn't fucking matter," I say. "It's my property."

One eyebrow raises. "You were on a tear to figure out who did this earlier."

Natalie steps forward and puts a hand on my arm. "It's okay."

The door clicks open, and Damon pushes inside. How the hell did she manage to get inside? I'm curious, but not enough to risk her safety.

"It's not okay. We're going home."

Her smile is sad. "Where is home? Gabriel and Avery's house? Upstairs?"

"A dorm room in Illinois," I counter, and her eyes widen. "Yeah, I know who you are. I know what you did. And I don't care. You're more important to me than a piece of ivory."

"More important than revenge?"

Yes. The word stalls in my throat. I've been waiting to do this for years. Since I was a child, helping Momma button her clothes and count out quarters at the laundromat.

Am I really willing to give that up for a woman I haven't known very long?

That hesitation may cost me everything.

Her expression firms. "I have to do this. For me. And for you."

Before I can argue, she steps into the ballroom. It looks almost spooky with every chandelier shining brightly with no people inside, as if it's a ghost party. The paintings from the auction hang on the wall. The gemstones and other items are there, too. Nothing has moved.

Damon makes a sweeping motion, looking at Natalie. "It's your show."

She glances at me, and in that gaze I see the swift gesture that knocks a piece over, I see plastic pieces spilling in my lap, I see my mother's head bobbing unnaturally on her shoulders.

"I didn't show up on the security scanner because I didn't come in after the party." She nods her head toward the gowns. "I was under her skirt. It smells like moths under there."

"Did you have prior knowledge they'd be there?" This from the lady fed.

"Nah, I had a plan to hide in that cabinet under the caterer's station. The gown was better. When everyone cleared out I took the bishop." A self-deprecating grimace. "I stole it."

"And where is it now?" Damon asks.

"Here." She nods her head toward her painting, then walks over. Except she doesn't stop at her painting. She stops at the next one. The one that looks like chaos. Paintings and nails and keys. She reaches over, through some sharp netting, and I think to myself she needs a tetanus shot. Then she pulls out the bishop. "I kept it here because I wanted it somewhere safe. Somewhere where I could have negotiating power against my step-father, but where he couldn't take it from me."

She looks down at the piece in her hand. Her thumb brushes over nine-hundred-year-old ivory. Then she holds it out to me. "It's yours. I'm sorry I ever took it."

"I'm not," I say, my voice thick. Fuck revenge. Fuck the nine-hundred-year-old past. I'm living and breathing and *hurting* at the realization that I might not get to keep her. "I'm glad you did it, so I could wake up and stop beating my head against history. And mostly so I could meet you."

Unshed tears brighten her dark eyes. She turns to the feds. "So there's your proof. Along with my statement on Norman Crawford. I hope it will be enough to make the arrest."

"If everything checks out," the boy fed says, sounding ominous. "We've been looking into Crawford for some time. But you understand that you don't have immunity here."

"Am I the only one who cares that no actual theft occurred?" I snap. "The chess piece stayed in the building. Not to mention I'm not pressing charges. Actually, you know what? I'm giving this as a gift. This bishop belongs to Natalie Lhuirs."

"A gift?" Damon says with a pretend-thoughtful look. I glare at him, but he ignores me, naturally. "A trade might make more sense. You won the bid on her painting, after all. I'm in charge of the auction, of course, and that sounds fair to me. You give her the bishop, and she gives you the painting."

Her eyes fill. "You bought my painting."

"Called in a bid while the auction was happening," Damon says.

"Like the city at night. Beauty and danger." It doesn't matter if Damon and the feds hear me spouting poetic bullshit. Doesn't matter if the whole city knows. "Yes, I bought your painting. I wanted every piece of you before I even knew your name."

"Anders." She takes a step toward me.

That's all the momentum I need. I pull her into my arms, fusing my lips to hers, drinking her in, this woman of black and gold, this priceless artifact of a million different facets. "Don't leave again, little thief. Stay and fight with me."

Chapter Fourteen

Natalie

Most of my memories come from a narrow, two-story townhouse. I made castles out of the room beneath the stairs. I imagined jungles in the four-foot square of overgrown weeds in our back patio. The cracked linoleum and threadbare carpet never bothered me. I suppose I didn't know any better. Now my mother lives in a house with beige carpet and beige walls. Everything new. They've lived here for years, but it still feels new—not lived in. It's never been my dream, but I know how much it means to my mom. She wanted this.

She dreamed about it. And now she has it.

For how long? Norman Crawford was taken into custody this morning. The charges focus on the theft of the chess piece for now, but they're hoping the subpoenas of his personal email and phone records give them leeway for even more. Corruption only touches the surface. He's been involved in some shady business with the state senator. What happens when Mom can't make the mortgage payment? She'll lose the house. She'll lose her dreams, and it won't matter that he hit her. It was the price she chose to pay. There's a stone the size of that chess piece in my throat. I don't want to face her. I have to face her. Squaring my shoulders, I cross the small brick pathway. I use the key to let myself inside. She's sitting on the leather couch that she oils every week, her manicured hands folded in her lap.

I sit down next to her, feeling like a stranger. "Mom."

Something flashes in her familiar eyes, something scary. "Don't."

"He was hurting you." The knot in my throat gets bigger, because I shouldn't have to convince her of this. She should be on my side. "He was hurting *me*. I had to do something."

"You lived in his house. You ate the food he bought. You drove around in the car he bought."

Tears prick my eyes. I pull aside the neck of my T-shirt, revealing the line of stitches. "He did this to me. There were bruises, too. They've mostly healed now, but I'll have this scar forever. How are you okay with that? You're my mother. You're supposed to protect me."

"And you would have been protected, if you'd been smart about it. That chess piece could have paid off your student loans and bought us a new house and SUV, and retirement besides."

Bile rises in my throat. "So you knew about it. I didn't want to believe that."

"Knew about it? It was my idea. Norman held on to that stupid thing, said it was worth a fortune but that it was too risky to sell it, too *recognizable*, he said. I said forget it. I'm not going to keep working at that dentist's office so we can grow old and live off his pension."

"What are you talking about? He held on to what?"

"The chess piece! And then he heard about the auction. A matched pair, from the same set. It would have been worth a fortune, and forget about the risk. We could go anywhere in the world."

My stomach turns over. I stand up, holding my hands across my middle, trying to avoid throwing up. "You're saying there are two of them."

"Not that it matters now. We'll never be able to sell it."

"Mom. Do you know where he got it from?"

"Probably the evidence room, where he found things sometimes. Oh, don't look at me that way. It wasn't doing anyone any good locked up behind a fence."

My head shakes back and forth. "No," I whisper. "That's not where he got it."

"How do you know?"

"Because I know how it was lost. A woman was walking home years ago. Someone attacked her in an alley. Raped her. Beat her." The same way he beat me. "She owned that chess piece."

For one electric second she looks as horrified as I feel. She looks like the mom I grew up with. The one I laughed and cried with. *You and me against the world.* And then her expression hardens. "You're making that up so you feel better about what you've done."

"I'm not—"

"I don't believe you." Her voice is shrill now.

My pulse beats heavy in my ears. "You *do* believe me. I can tell."

In the quiet I feel every *Hosanna* we've sung in the church pews together. I feel every hopeful, heartfelt beat of the song. And then the notes drift away. "Natalie." Her voice sounds thick. "I'm too old to start over. Too tired. I *can't* believe you."

"You're supposed to protect me." The words come out soft. *You're my mother.* "We're family."

"I'm sorry," she says, her voice choked. "He's my family now. We're going to sort this out… and we're going to live our lives. Without you."

There are tears in her eyes now, and I don't want to feel bad for her, but I do. That's the terrible part about love—caring even when the other person stops. There's a crack somewhere deep inside me, the kind that runs through a single piece of ivory, the kind of scar that stays with you until the day you die.

* * * *

Anders

She asked me to stay in the car.

I should be inside with her.

She asked me to stay in the car.

I should be inside with her, damn it. My more possessive side wins out, and I give her a soft knock of warning on the nondescript white door before entering. As soon as I see the look on her face, I know I made the right decision—probably waited too long. She looks devastated, facing the woman who could only be her mother. They look alike. The same petite build. The same straight, dark hair. The same pretty eyes. That's only the packaging, though. I have some experience reading people, making that split-second call, and I have a feeling these two are completely different on the inside.

"There a problem," I say, wrapping my arm around Natalie's waist.

Natalie's face twists, and I can tell she's holding back tears.

"Anders."

"You," her mother gasps, and I realize that her mother was more than a victim. She was an accomplice. And that makes me despise her. She hurt Natalie. No one gets to do that, not even her mother. Especially not her mother.

I tighten my hold on Natalie's slender, shivering body. "You have something of mine, I believe. Don't bother pretending. We already have Crawford's statement."

Resentment. Anger. Fear. She doesn't want to give me the piece, but she won't have a choice. Not that it would help her with the feds closing in. They already have her husband on a dozen different charges, including fraud and perjury. They even tacked on tax evasion for good measure. There's no escape for him.

And even if there was, if he somehow slipped through the legal net, I'd be there waiting for him the day he got out. Not as revenge for my mother, though she deserves that.

It would be for every woman he hurt along the way, including Natalie.

I have what you could call unconventional ethics for a doctor. It comes from working outside the law. You heal enough people who are afraid of authority, you learn it can be dangerous in the wrong hands.

After a long moment, Natalie's mother disappears into her bedroom. She comes back holding a nine-hundred-year-old chess piece I've never seen before.

I've only heard about this one.

I hold it to the light between thumb and forefinger, studying the blunt carving. "Such a small thing to destroy so many lives. Imagine how much trouble it's caused over the centuries. The creator probably had no idea what would happen."

"Such a worthless thing to keep around," her mother says, shooting venom at me.

There are two pieces remaining for one historic set. Both bishops. My mother kept one in her pocket when she went out. My father kept the other one. For safekeeping. Except it didn't keep her safe. Hell, it's just a piece of ivory. Old ivory, carved ivory. It can't do a damned thing to protect her. I take it without another word—no thanks and no accusations.

I always figured someone would want the other half. Maybe because they had a love of old chess pieces. Or maybe it was good old-fashioned greed. Like Damon said, money's the one human constant. He might not be that far off the mark.

Natalie makes it to the car before a sob wracks her body.

"Sorry," she says, shuddering with the effort to hold it in.

She turns away, but I pull her back. We're standing in the sunlight in the middle of suburbia, where they have no fucking clue what goes on behind closed doors. I don't care if they're looking. I don't care who sees.

I take her face in both my hands. "You go ahead and cry, Natalie. You lost your mother. I lost mine, too. Maybe in different ways, but it's the fucking same to the child inside us. So go ahead and cry. I'm here. I'm here with you. I'll be here when you're done."

She fights it for one more heartrending second, and then she breaks down. Her sobs echo off the pristine hedges and bright white curbs. I hold her against my chest, absorbing her pain, feeling it with her. The curtains flicker in that lifeless house—and then go still again. Her mother probably has a million excuses in her head, but she made her choice long before this day.

It feels completely natural to drive her to Avery and Gabriel's house on the outskirts of the city. The last time I took her there she was unconscious from pain, her body bruised, bleeding into the backseat. Today she's sitting upright, mostly healed on the outside—her heart completely battered. There's a shell-shocked look in her eyes like the kind a man has after a gunfight.

Trauma doesn't always break the skin, but it always leaves a scar.

I call ahead to let them know I'm coming. Her eyes don't blink when I murmur into the phone. I don't think she's even aware of her surroundings.

The gate opens as we pull in. Gabriel's waiting at the front door, his expression severe. Avery looks anxious. Natalie's dark eyes don't register anything. If she were the city at night, it would be full of thick fog— impenetrable, opaque. She follows as I lead her upstairs, apparently docile, though I think it has less to do with obedience and more to do with self-preservation.

In the bedroom I undress her slowly, checking each healed-over wound. It's always like this when I see her naked body—part of me wanting to heal her, part of me wanting to fuck her. Then I draw a hot bath with plush towels draped over the sides so she doesn't slip. I drop in a palm-full of salts, and the scent of rose rises from the tub.

Steam thickens the air. Little droplets cling to her lips, her nose, her eyelashes. A flush touches her cheeks. I don't think it's only coming from the warmth. The sensations, the smells, the sound of rushing water—it's bringing her to the present.

I lean to kiss her forehead. It's chaste enough, except that I can't quite resist the swipe of my tongue along her skin. That brings her back to the present, too.

Her dark eyes widen as I undress. This body she wanted to paint in white and beige and blue—with streaks of red, incongruous, this violence inside me, this rage. It's bared to her in the lukewarm light of the evening. "Do you know," I say, tone almost casual as I unbuckle my belt, "that violence has been inside me a long time. As long as I can remember. I thought I needed it."

She doesn't answer, but I still hear the understanding in her voice in the observatory.

Do you know that bullets actually sear the skin? Cook it hard and fast until it's as black as the bottom of that bread Avery made tonight. The first thing I have to do, before I can even pull out the metal, is cut away the burnt skin. Slice it off like it's the part of a steak you don't want to eat.

Anyone else would turn away from me. Everyone else *did* turn away from me. Even my friends, Gabriel and Damon, they think this is who I am. Like the doctor thing is a hobby.

And I suppose, for most of my life, it was.

My real goal was finding the man who hurt my mother. Killing him. I needed to keep my heart hard enough to do that. Couldn't let myself care about the babies and the mothers of the world, not if I had to kill a man in cold blood.

She saw right through me.

I didn't like that at the time, but I'm baring myself on purpose now. I push down my briefs. Then I'm standing naked in the gleaming bathroom.

"My father searched the west side of Tanglewood for two days before they found her. Brought her home. Called the cops. She wasn't able to give a good description. Hardly ever talked again, so of course nothing was ever done. The law failed her, and I never thought to trust it again."

She blinks up at me, and the uncertainty in her eyes makes my chest ache.

I brush her hair over her shoulder. "As soon as I had any money, I put out feelers on the black market—waiting, waiting, waiting for the bishop to show up. It never did, and I was starting to lose hope. I thought someone must have it who loved chess—otherwise, why not sell it? So I decided to put the matching piece for sale. Whoever owned the piece would want it. They would kill for it."

It could be a scene out of a ballroom, the way I hold her hand high, helping her step into the tub. Except that neither of us are wearing any clothes. Her breasts make points in her silhouette, and I fight myself not to touch her. My cock throbs. It feels arctic in the steamy air, when it really wants to be inside Natalie. I arrange us in the water so that she's sitting in front of me, tucked between my legs, my cock nestled against her back. *Ignore it.* I grit my teeth against the slippery friction—*God.* Her head leans back on my shoulder, and she relaxes a fraction.

"What I didn't realize," I say, running my hand along her arms, "is that the person kept it not for a love of chess, but because they were afraid of the heat. It still did the trick, though. Alone, it's worth a lot of money. Together? They're worth a fortune."

"I'm sorry," she says on a sigh, but she isn't pulling away from me.

"Don't be. You were a victim as much as my mother."

Something warm lands on my forearm, and I realize she's crying. Considering the circumstances, that's actually a good thing. Far better than being numb. The hot water, the touch of skin, all of it's thawing her out. I know how it feels to be encased in ice. For so long, encased in ice. She's the one who set me free. I was the one who bathed her, but in those moments, with my cock hard, my body shuddering with desire, she thawed me out.

I turn my head to the side, press a kiss to her temple. "You were the one who called the FBI in, and I was so fucking pissed when I realized what you'd done. Because I didn't trust them. And the idea that you would turn yourself in—I was furious at you. Only you were strong enough to trust the system, in a city where power rules above the law, in a building owned by a criminal—you believed, and it worked."

She presses back, and I can't hold back a groan.

The slender body in front of me begins to shake, and I make a *shushing* sound. I stroke my hand along her hair, her arms, her sides. Then I realize she's not crying. She's laughing.

"I don't know how—" She breaks off into hysterical peals, tears glistening on her cheeks. "I don't know how we can talk about this while you're—while you're so clearly—"

A reluctant smile tugs at my lips. "Are you making fun of my cock?"

This sets her off again, and she dissolves into helpless, tear-soaked giggles. "God," she says. "What a mess. What a *mess*. Why are you still taking care of me? I'd have thought you'd be halfway across Tanglewood to get away from me, after you got your chess piece back."

"You didn't think you were getting rid of me that easily, did you?"

She sighs, snuggling back against me. "I hoped not."

"Me and my very hard, very solid piece of wood aren't finished with you."

That earns me a wriggle of her pretty heart-shaped bottom. Water sloshes against my cock. I fight myself not to push my cock against her back, to rub against her skin until I shoot white cum along her spine. I fight myself not to grasp her hips and impale her on my cock—to move her with my hands up and down, fucking her with the force of pure gravity, until I hold her hips down and come.

As much as I want to fuck her, there will be time for that later. Time when she doesn't have to wonder if I only want her for her body. I need her to understand that the chess piece doesn't change a damn thing. I flip her over so she's kneeling between my legs, the water in wild waves between us.

"I need you," I tell her, "to let me heal you. And to heal me, too."

Her dark eyes reflect caution and sorrow—and God, so much hope it hurts to see. "You do?"

I grasp her hand, hot and slick from the bath, and place it over my heart. "Here." I shove it down where my cock bobs obscenely out of the water. "And here." Her fist squeezes, and I grunt.

Confidence gleams golden in those midnight eyes. "Right here."

"It hurts. Only you can make it better."

She doesn't leave me cold and aching—not for very long, anyway. Her hands and her eyes and her mouth, all of them heal bruises deep in my goddamn soul. They make me feel like a whole person again, not only body parts walking around. They make me into a man.

Chapter Fifteen

Anders

The bouncer nods at me as I head through the front door. I take the stairs two at a time, eager to wash the stench of the street off me. Disinfectant can only do so much. I toss my bag into the door by my room, ducking into the bathroom to clean up. A shower makes me marginally more human. I'm wearing only a towel when I step into my bedroom.

On my bed there's a woman.

She doesn't glance up from the textbook that's open in front of her. "I thought the dorm rooms at U of I were small, but this is something else." Then she does look up, and her dark eyes turn wide at the sight of my half-naked body. Or maybe it's the thickening cock tenting the towel that makes her look wary. It *has* been two weeks. "There's barely room to walk around."

"I thought you were coming tomorrow."

"Class let out early, and I figured, why spend the night wishing I were here? That was before I knew about the twin-size bed. Seriously, how do you sleep in this thing?"

Affecting a casual manner, I walk over to my dresser. I'm turned away from her when I drop the towel, but I still hear her gasp. "We could grab a room at The Rose and Crown Motel."

She makes a sound of distaste. "No, thank you."

I turn and walk toward her. She averts her eyes, but there's a telltale darkening on her cheeks. My little artist still blushes when she sees a man in the nude. I bend over her, and she leans back. I'm naked and aching for her. She's fully dressed. It's the exact opposite of how we were when I cared for her. "Maybe you can give me a bath."

"You just showered," she says, half laughing.

"Well then, I'm out of ideas."

She glances up at me, a little shy, a little knowing. "Are you?"

Sex. That's what she's suggesting, and lord knows my cock is ready. I imagine I'll take her two, maybe three times before I finally have enough control to converse with her. Before that there's something I need to show her. Something I need to ask. Nervousness tightens my stomach, but I reach over to my side table. It's not hard, because she's right—this room is fucking small. It was never meant for two people. Maybe not even one. It won't matter soon.

I hold out a folded-up packet of papers. "I have one more idea."

She opens the papers. Those beautiful eyes widen. "What's this?"

There's doubt in my throat. Or maybe it's hope, like Gabriel said once. Maybe it's love. "Travel. Since neither of us has a place to settle down, we can explore a little first."

"Oh, my God. Anders."

That's not exactly a *yes*. "I thought… Hell, this might be the wrong idea, but I thought we could go to the Philippines. They need doctors there right now. Even more than the west side, which is saying something. I thought I could do some good there."

"Yes," she says. "I'm coming with you."

"And I thought you could paint. Not all the time. There'd be some traveling. And some… living in tents. It's not exactly comfortable. But it's…"

"It's human. It's living."

"Exactly." It's dying, too. Less dying, though, if I can help. "Though we could probably visit some regular places, if you want. London and Greece and—"

She throws her arms around my neck, and I stagger back, catching her. Enough talking. Her warmth and her weight, it's too much for my hard cock to handle. I can only kiss her and touch her. Only reach down to open her jeans. Then I'm inside her, thrusting, fighting, struggling to get deeper. *It's human.* That's the one constant. Not money. Desire to connect, to get closer, to fuse my body to hers. And when I'm all the way there, pulsing deep, feeling her thrash under me, ripple around me, I know that this, *this*, is finally living.

Sign up for the 1001 Dark Nights Newsletter
and be entered to win a Tiffany Key necklace.

There's a contest every month!

Go to www.1001DarkNights.com to subscribe.

As a bonus, all subscribers can download
FIVE FREE exclusive books!

Discover 1001 Dark Nights Collection Seven

For more information, go to www.1001DarkNights.com.

THE BISHOP by Skye Warren
A Tanglewood Novella

TAKEN WITH YOU by Carrie Ann Ryan
A Fractured Connections Novella

DRAGON LOST by Donna Grant
A Dark Kings Novella

SEXY LOVE by Carly Phillips
A Sexy Series Novella

PROVOKE by Rachel Van Dyken
A Seaside Pictures Novella

RAFE by Sawyer Bennett
An Arizona Vengeance Novella

THE NAUGHTY PRINCESS by Claire Contreras
A Sexy Royals Novella

THE GRAVEYARD SHIFT by Darynda Jones
A Charley Davidson Novella

CHARMED by Lexi Blake
A Masters and Mercenaries Novella

SACRIFICE OF DARKNESS by Alexandra Ivy
A Guardians of Eternity Novella

THE QUEEN by Jen Armentrout
A Wicked Novella

BEGIN AGAIN by Jennifer Probst
A Stay Novella

VIXEN by Rebecca Zanetti
A Dark Protectors/Rebels Novella

SLASH by Laurelin Paige
A Slay Series Novella

THE DEAD HEAT OF SUMMER by Heather Graham
A Krewe of Hunters Novella

WILD FIRE by Kristen Ashley
A Chaos Novella

MORE THAN PROTECT YOU by Shayla Black
A More Than Words Novella

LOVE SONG by Kylie Scott
A Stage Dive Novella

CHERISH ME by J. Kenner
A Stark Ever After Novella

SHINE WITH ME by Kristen Proby
A With Me in Seattle Novella

And new from Blue Box Press:

TEASE ME by J. Kenner
A Stark International Novel

The Pawn

By Skye Warren

Now Available

The price of survival…

Gabriel Miller swept into my life like a storm. He tore down my father with cold retribution, leaving him penniless in a hospital bed. I quit my private all-girl's college to take care of the only family I have left.

There's one way to save our house, one thing I have left of value.

My virginity.

A forbidden auction…

Gabriel appears at every turn. He seems to take pleasure in watching me fall. Other times he's the only kindness in a brutal underworld.

Except he's playing a deeper game than I know. Every move brings us together, every secret rips us apart. And when the final piece is played, only one of us can be left standing.

"Skye Warren's THE PAWN is a triumph of intrigue, angst, and sensual drama. I was clenching everything. Gabriel and Avery sucked me in from the first few paragraphs and never let go." – New York Times bestselling author Annabel Joseph

* * * *

Wind whips around my ankles, flapping the bottom of my black trench coat. Beads of moisture form on my eyelashes. In the short walk from the cab to the stoop, my skin has slicked with humidity left by the rain.

Carved vines and ivy leaves decorate the ornate wooden door.

I have some knowledge of antique pieces, but I can't imagine the price tag on this one—especially exposed to the elements and the whims of vandals. I suppose even criminals know enough to leave the Den alone.

Officially the Den is a gentlemen's club, the old-world kind with cigars and private invitations. Unofficially it's a collection of the most powerful men in Tanglewood. Dangerous men. Criminals, even if they wear a suit while breaking the law.

A heavy brass knocker in the shape of a fierce lion warns away any visitors. I'm desperate enough to ignore that warning. My heart thuds in my chest and expands out, pulsing in my fingers, my toes. Blood rushes through my ears, drowning out the whoosh of traffic behind me.

I grasp the thick ring and knock—once, twice.

Part of me fears what will happen to me behind that door. A bigger part of me is afraid the door won't open at all. I can't see any cameras set into the concrete enclave, but they have to be watching. Will they recognize me? I'm not sure it would help if they did. Probably best that they see only a desperate girl, because that's all I am now.

The softest scrape comes from the door. Then it opens.

I'm struck by his eyes, a deep amber color—like expensive brandy and almost translucent. My breath catches in my throat, lips frozen against words like *please* and *help*. Instinctively I know they won't work; this isn't a man given to mercy. The tailored cut of his shirt, its sleeves carelessly rolled up, tells me he'll extract a price. One I can't afford to pay.

There should have been a servant, I thought. A butler. Isn't that what fancy gentlemen's clubs have? Or maybe some kind of a security guard. Even our house had a housekeeper answer the door—at least, before. Before we fell from grace.

Before my world fell apart.

The man makes no move to speak, to invite me in or turn me away. Instead he stares at me with vague curiosity, with a trace of pity, the way one might watch an animal in the zoo. That might be how the whole world looks to these men, who have more money than God, more power than the president.

That might be how I looked at the world, before.

My throat feels tight, as if my body fights this move, even while my mind knows it's the only option. "I need to speak with Damon Scott."

Scott is the most notorious loan shark in the city. He deals with large sums of money, and nothing less will get me through this. We have been introduced, and he left polite society by the time I was old enough to attend events regularly. There were whispers, even then, about the young man with ambition. Back then he had ties to the underworld—and now he's its king.

One thick eyebrow rises. "What do you want with him?"

A sense of familiarity fills the space between us even though I know we haven't met. This man is a stranger, but he looks at me as if he wants to know me. He looks at me as if he already does. There's an intensity to his eyes when they sweep over my face, as firm and as telling as a touch.

"I need…" My heart thuds as I think about all the things I need—a rewind button. One person in the city who doesn't hate me by name alone. "I need a loan."

He gives me a slow perusal, from the nervous slide of my tongue along my lips to the high neckline of my clothes. I tried to dress professionally—a black cowl-necked sweater and pencil skirt. His strange amber gaze unbuttons my coat, pulls away the expensive cotton, tears off the fabric of my bra and panties. He sees right through me, and I shiver as a ripple of awareness runs over my skin.

I've met a million men in my life. Shaken hands. Smiled. I've never felt as seen through as I do right now. Never felt like someone has turned me inside out, every dark secret exposed to the harsh light. He sees my weaknesses, and from the cruel set of his mouth, he likes them.

His lids lower. "And what do you have for collateral?"

Nothing except my word. That wouldn't be worth anything if he knew my name. I swallow past the lump in my throat. "I don't know."

Nothing.

He takes a step forward, and suddenly I'm crowded against the brick wall beside the door, his large body blocking out the warm light from inside. He feels like a furnace in front of me, the heat of him in sharp contrast to the cold brick at my back. "What's your name, girl?"

The word *girl* is a slap in the face. I force myself not to flinch, but it's hard. Everything about him overwhelms me—his size, his low voice. "I'll tell Mr. Scott my name."

In the shadowed space between us, his smile spreads, white and taunting. The pleasure that lights his strange yellow eyes is almost sensual, as if I caressed him. "You'll have to get past me."

My heart thuds. He likes that I'm challenging him, and God, that's even worse. What if I've already failed? I'm free-falling, tumbling, turning over without a single hope to anchor me. Where will I go if he turns me away? What will happen to my father?

"Let me go," I whisper, but my hope fades fast.

His eyes flash with warning. "Little Avery James, all grown up."

A small gasp resounds in the space between us. He already knows my name. That means he knows who my father is. He knows what he's done. Denials rush to my throat, pleas for understanding. The hard set of his eyes, the broad strength of his shoulders tells me I won't find any mercy here.

I square my shoulders. I'm desperate but not broken. "If you know my name, you know I have friends in high places. Connections. A history in this city. That has to be worth something. That's my collateral."

Those connections might not even take my call, but I have to try something. I don't know if it will be enough for a loan or even to get me through the door. Even so, a faint feeling of family pride rushes over my skin. Even if he turns me away, I'll hold my head high.

Golden eyes study me. Something about the way he said *little Avery James* felt familiar, but I've never seen this man. At least I don't think we've met. Something about the otherworldly glow of those eyes whispers to me, like a melody I've heard before.

On his driver's license it probably says something mundane, like brown. But that word can never encompass the way his eyes seem almost luminous, orbs of amber that hold the secrets of the universe. *Brown* can never describe the deep golden hue of them, the indelible opulence in his fierce gaze.

"Follow me," he says.

Relief courses through me, flooding numb limbs, waking me up enough that I wonder what I'm doing here. These aren't men, they're animals. They're predators, and I'm prey. Why would I willingly walk inside?

What other choice do I have?

I step over the veined marble threshold.

The man closes the door behind me, shutting out the rain and the traffic, the entire city disappeared in one soft turn of the lock. Without another word he walks down the hall, deeper into the shadows. I hurry to follow him, my chin held high, shoulders back, for all the world as if I were an invited guest. Is this how the gazelle feels when she runs over the plains, a study in grace, poised for her slaughter?

The entire world goes black behind the staircase, only breath, only bodies in the dark. Then he opens another thick wooden door, revealing a dimly lit room of cherrywood and cut crystal, of leather and smoke. Barely I see dark eyes, dark suits. Dark men.

I have the sudden urge to hide behind the man with the golden eyes. He's wide and tall, with hands that could wrap around my waist. He's a giant of a man, rough-hewn and hard as stone.

Except he's not here to protect me.

He could be the most dangerous of all.

About Skye Warren

Skye Warren is the New York Times bestselling author of dangerous romance. Her books have sold over one million copies. She makes her home in Texas with her loving family, sweet dogs, and evil cat.

For more information, visit https://www.skyewarren.com.

Discover 1001 Dark Nights

For more information, go to www.1001DarkNights.com.

ENCHANTED by Lexi Blake
TAKE THE BRIDE by Carly Phillips
INDULGE ME by J. Kenner
THE KING by Jennifer L. Armentrout
QUIET MAN by Kristen Ashley
ABANDON by Rachel Van Dyken
THE OPEN DOOR by Laurelin Paige
CLOSER by Kylie Scott
SOMETHING JUST LIKE THIS by Jennifer Probst
BLOOD NIGHT by Heather Graham
TWIST OF FATE by Jill Shalvis
MORE THAN PLEASURE YOU by Shayla Black
WONDER WITH ME by Kristen Proby
THE DARKEST ASSASSIN by Gena Showalter

Discover Blue Box Press

TAME ME by J. Kenner
TEMPT ME by J. Kenner
DAMIEN by J. Kenner
TEASE ME by J. Kenner
REAPER by Larissa Ione
THE SURRENDER GATE by Christopher Rice
SERVICING THE TARGET by Cherise Sinclair

On Behalf of 1001 Dark Nights,

Liz Berry, M.J. Rose, and Jillian Stein would like to thank ~

Steve Berry
Doug Scofield
Benjamin Stein
Kim Guidroz
InkSlinger PR
Dan Slater
Asha Hossain
Chris Graham
Chelle Olson
Kasi Alexander
Jessica Johns
Dylan Stockton
Richard Blake
and Simon Lipskar